A thought came to King
that brought the chill of ice.

"Mjollnir. The Hammer of Thor. Must be nearly a cubic kilometer of rock in that asteroid."

"Could they really aim this thing at Earth—and hit it?" asked the dwarf.

"Yes, if their calculations are good." King's throat felt dry. "The impact of a thing like this could wipe the slate clean of life all over the Earth."

"Do you think Slade realizes that?"

"He might not. Or maybe he does. And maybe he just doesn't damn well care. . . . "

Ace Science Fiction Books by Wynne Whiteford

THOR'S HAMMER
BREATHING SPACE ONLY (coming in January 1986)

THOR'S HAMMER

WYNNE WHITEFORD

ACE SCIENCE FICTION BOOKS
NEW YORK

This Ace Science Fiction book
contains the complete text of the
original edition. It has been
completely reset in a typeface designed
for easy reading, and was printed from
new film.

THOR'S HAMMER

An Ace Science Fiction Book / published by arrangement with
the author

PRINTING HISTORY
Cory & Collins edition / 1983
Ace Science Fiction edition / November 1985

ISBN: 0-441-80755-0

Ace Science Fiction Books are published by
The Berkley Publishing Group,
200 Madison Avenue, New York, New York 10016.

PRINTED IN THE UNITED STATES OF AMERICA

ONE

Tension. King could feel it building within him minute by minute. It did not arise from any anxiety about possible danger in the coming landing, for no accidents happened to space shuttles these days, and he had been through enough touchdowns to be thoroughly familiar with the routine.

He had felt the first hint of contagious uneasiness when Ashman had made his satellite-relayed call to him from Head Office. Uneasiness was a rare state now that human moods could be so smoothly controlled, but it had been there in the hologram of Max Ashman, startling and unmistakable.

It had sparked an atavistic insecurity in King. The feeling had not come from anything Ashman had said—rather, it was generated by speculation about what he had *not* said.

The shuttle adopted a shallower angle on its approach path, the thin upper air shrieking over its knife-blade wings. The turgid drama on the screens raced to a frenetic conclusion, closing scenes accelerated, chopped short as the computer edited them to adjust to the estimated time of arrival. The credits rolled up over the final shot too swiftly to be absorbed, and were replaced by a pilot's view of the landing relayed from a camera in the nose of the craft.

Leaning forward against his seat-belt, King lifted his brief case and rested it across his knees, looking at it thoughtfully for a few seconds before opening it. It was of black leatheroid, engraved in gold with his name:

**KINGSTON HANNAN
ASTROGOLD CORPORATION**

He glanced over his shoulder, but the high backs of the seats hid the few other passengers of the shuttle. He slid his compact video recorder from the case, and played back Ashman's call, frowning as he concentrated on the sharp image on the small screen, looking for something he might have missed the first time.

Ashman was seated at his massive golden desk, the gilt emblem of the Astrogold Corporation shining on the dark wall behind him. Somehow, he did not seem to radiate his usual aura of easy power. Between his heavy brows was a taut, vertical crease that King hadn't noticed before. His voice came thinly but clearly from the recorder.

"King, I want you back here straight away."

King heard his own voice on the recording. "Hell, Max, I need another twenty hours to set up the launcher programs."

"Forget what's happening there. Something vital has come through! I've had the shuttle pushed ahead of schedule to pick you up. Say in three hours."

"But what's happened?"

Ashman shook his head. "Tell you about it when you're here."

That had been the end of the telecast. Less than twenty seconds of it. King ran it through again, then switched off the recorder and slipped it back into his brief case, staring out through the double vitrite port.

The shuttle was biting into thicker air, now, and the nose was lifting slightly, bringing the sharp titanium-alloy wings into a higher angle of attack to kill some of its forward speed. Waves of dull red heat pulsed back from the leading edge. King stared morosely at the red light beside the screen of the videophone on the back of the seat in front of him, then switched his attention to the external view again.

Far down below the blue and white air, the sea gleamed in the sunlight like a sheet of buffed metal. He was home. He tried to hold the thought in the front of his mind, to allay the premonition of danger that had begun seeping into him. The scene outside didn't help him much. From this height, there was nothing to show that the Earth had any life on it.

He kept his head across near the side of the port, so he could see as far forward as possible towards their line of flight. The glow of heat flared angrily along the wing, and ahead, under the dappled carpet of cloud, the metallic sheen of the sea dulled along the horizon with a paint-smear of land.

The red light in front of him changed to green, and he immediately picked up the videophone and punched out a series of remembered digits. A girl's face appeared on the small screen, a doll face under a swirl of lilac hair.

"Astrogold," she said. King knew it was a computer-controlled recording, but he answered as if it were a direct conversation.

"King Hannan. Could I speak to Max Ashman?"

"One moment, please." Music, and a vortex of colored light-patterns on the screen. Then, after a few seconds, Ashman's face appeared, this time against a background of towering gantries and handling machines.

"Coming in now, Max," said King. "Can you fill in any more details for me?"

Ashman began speaking before King had finished. "This is a recording. I'll be unavailable for a short time. Leave your message and I'll get back to you." His image vanished and blue and gold bands rippled across the screen, overlaid by the Astrogold logo and the words "speak now."

"See you, Max," said King irritably. He punched out another long series of digits on the phone, again from memory. This time the delay was longer, then a girl with a heart-shaped face and enamelled red hair looked out at him from the screen with large, green-outlined eyes. She smiled as she recognized him.

"Hi, King! Where are you?"

"Coming in on the shuttle. Good to see you again, Moya. Have to see Ashman first, then I'll be over."

"Wasn't expecting you back yet."

"Some emergency's come up. Don't know what it is, yet, but Max wanted me back here right away."

"But weren't you out at L5, or somewhere?"

"Yes. Must be big trouble."

"And there was no one here to handle whatever it was? Must be nice to be the chief's right-hand operator."

"Might be something—delicate. Max and I understand each other pretty well."

"I know. Kids together, weren't you?" She smiled, lifting one corner of her mouth and the opposite eyebrow in an expression that was uniquely hers. "I got all the data about the two of you from Max's girl. You both showed early promise, right? And you both grew up as products of the same school of hormonal engineering. Right?"

"Well, yes. But how did this come up?"

"Max's girl Helga and I have become quite friendly. I met her when we were both going to Gazelles."

"Gazelles? Can you fill me in on that?"

"Very upgrade glamor factory. Expensive, but worth it. They induce selective late growth in long bones, things like that. Train you in altered body rhythms, everything." Her smile grew mischievous. "You'll find you won't be able to tower over me quite so much."

He grinned. "Be over to give you a verdict after I've seen Max."

Her smile faded, and her eyes seemed to darken. "Be home for good this time?"

He shrugged his shoulders. "Hope so, Moya."

"Hope so? Listen, just tell Max you simply *can't* go off Earth again. After all, when ninety-five per cent of people don't work at all, and have an easy life, why should *you* have to spend your time in gruesome places?"

He hesitated. He had explained to her before about responsibility. His training, education and hormonal modification had been long and costly, costly in a number of ways. Right now, he didn't feel like giving her the old lecture on integrity. Instead, he looked at his watch.

"Moya, there are a couple of other calls I have to make. I'll see you as soon as I'm through with Max."

She kissed her fingers and blew across them towards the video camera. He smiled, made a clutching movement in the air before him, and held his own hand to his lips.

As the picture left the screen, he sat staring out of the window at the unrolling continent below the tattered veil of clouds. He had no one else to call at the moment, but he wanted time to think.

Max Ashman glanced at his watch as he brought his aircar down in a straight, shallow incline over the soaring towers of the city. Like all cities built mainly in the 21st century, it lacked the deep, narrow street canyons that characterized earlier metropolitan centers. Developing in the aircar era, it had its skyscrapers spaced well apart across the plains, reflected in the wide canals where container vessels and hovercraft freighters came in from the sea.

Ahead of him, the 110-story tower of Astrogold was still one of the highest buildings in the city—when it had been built, in the boom period fifty years ago, it had been taller than any structure within sight of it. The metal sheathing the outside of it was plated in real gold, in an ostentatious display of the corporation's insolent power.

Astrogold had ridden the crest of the first wave of expansion of mining companies into the Asteroid Belt, and the gold on the walls of its headquarters had been mined cheaply on metallic asteroids far beyond the orbit of Mars. Gold was cheap these days, but half a century ago it had still been a symbol of opulence and stability.

Ashman switched on his videophone, pressing one of a series of buttons that opened direct channels. A man's face looked out at him from the small screen placed high on the instrument panel, close to his line of sight forward.

"Any sign?" asked Ashman.

"Be down in a couple of minutes. Fifteen more for him to get here on the linduc."

"Right. Buzz me when you see him, then bring him straight to my office."

"Will do."

Ashman levelled the aircar and took it in to a practiced landing on the second-highest flange surrounding the Astrogold Tower. He strode across the flange towards the golden wall, touching a small control on his wrist-watch band to emit the personal signal to open a sliding door that gave him access almost directly to his large office, with its floor-to-ceiling, polarized windows giving an immense vista of city, plains, canals and the distant arm of the sea.

The unobtrusive name-board on the huge golden desk read MAX ASHMAN, MANAGING DIRECTOR. In the days when the Corporation was soaring like a rocket, that would have been a title of overpowering prestige. It sometimes annoyed Ashman a little to reflect that he was probably the most able managing director the organization had ever possessed, but with the relative decline of the corporation the charisma attending its most powerful position had inevitably waned. Still, he reflected, today's world did not provide the right economic climate for supermen—or for the general recognition of supermen, even though they might exist.

Seated behind his desk, he passed his hand over the control of his intercom. His secretary's dark face looked questioningly out from a hologram cube above the end of his desk.

"Jaya," he said, "find out if both senior directors will be available in fifteen minutes or so."

She nodded briskly without speaking, and her image vanished. Ashman turned and studied a run of production figures on a VDT until a buzz sounded on his direct-line video. The face of the man waiting at the space terminal looked out at him.

"He just got out of the linduc, Chief. Just picking up some luggage."

"Right, Baz. How does he look?"

"Big fellow, about your build, a bit darker."

Ashman had to use conscious control to keep the bleak look out of his eyes. Why was he surrounded by idiots? "I know what he looks like, Baz—never mind, just bring him straight here."

"Will do, Chief."

As he broke the connection, Ashman glanced across at a small, violet light flashing near his intercom. He reached for it.

"Yes?"

His secretary looked at him from the hologram on the end of his desk again. "It's Helga. Have you time for a word with her?"

"Put her on."

The polaroid windows darkened, and a section of his office lit up with a three-dimensional hologram image of a tall woman in a long, silvery dress that clung skin-tight in places as she moved, apparently by some electrostatic effect. Her hair had a central parting, one side of it black, the other side platinum.

"Hi, Max. Just had a call from Moya. You know, King Hannan's girl—"

"I know," he put in quickly.

"It seems King called her from the shuttle. She wants him to stay on Earth instead of letting himself be raced off to some frontier outpost again. What are his chances?"

"I'm not sure, Helga. All I can say is—I'll do what I can."

"Thanks. She's a nice kid." She smiled. "See you."

"See you, Helga," he replied.

As her image vanished, and the polarized windows returned the outside scene to its normal brightness,

Ashman sat for a few seconds with his expression blank. Then a sudden smile twisted his lips.

He reached again for the intercom. "Jaya, see if you can get hold of the two senior directors now—before King Hannan arrives."

"Right," she said, and vanished. He sat back waiting, brooding.

As King Hannan stepped out on to the terminal platform from the linear induction train, he glanced along the line of parked cars beyond the barrier and picked out the golden machine with the Astrogold symbol on its side. As he looked at it, the man inside it spoke into a microphone, then emerged, waving to King.

He reached his side as King was about to retrieve his luggage, and at once took the larger bag.

"King Hannan? I'm Baz. I'll take you straight to the Chief." He flicked a lock of auburn hair from his eyes.

"Good."

An obvious part-timer, King thought as they walked towards the gate in the barrier. They had a lighthearted, undedicated look about them. He could see how Baz had so easily picked him out—the rest of the people on the shuttle had been vacationers who had saved up for the experience of a trip into space, and King had been the only one who had looked as if he were still operating on a schedule.

Baz handled the aircar smoothly enough. Relaxing, King looked ahead at the city. Every time he came to it, its skyline seemed to have changed. New towers thrust higher into the clear, pollution-free blue of the sky, and wider landing-flanges seemed to gird some of the others.

"Been with Astrogold long?" he asked.

"Three, four months. Saving up for an amphibian, you know? Want to have a look around the islands."

"Which ones?"

"Pacific, you know? Always wanted to see them."

"You'll like them. Historic. Some of the few places that haven't changed much in the last century."

"Don't know if *that* aspect appeals to me much. I

mean, we've got to keep moving forward, haven't we? The Chief always says that.''

"Ah, yes." Ashman would probably call it motivating his staff. King wondered if there was any way of hinting to Baz that his Chief's concept of moving forward might be vastly different from his. After a side-long glance at the younger man's happily enthusiastic face, he decided to leave the situation alone.

They passed over a huge, multi-winged parking structure that had not been there when King had last traveled this way, and a hectic amusement park where ant-streams of tiny, brightly colored vehicles swirled in a complex pattern, apparently spinning through the air on controlled paths. Beyond, a new, transparent dome enclosed a transplanted tropical hideaway with palm-shaded beaches around a turquoise lagoon.

Change! It came faster and faster, as if it had become a goal in itself. In a world where most people were paid not to work, it seemed unnecessary to King. Yet *was* it?

He was different from the people down there. He had long range and short range goals. Without those, perhaps he, too, would need a frenzy of pointless change.

The gleam of the Astrogold Tower ahead of them brought his mind back to the present moment. That unfamiliar feeling of insecurity chilled him again as he tried to imagine what kind of threat could have rocked the seemingly unshakeable poise of Max Ashman.

TWO

On the 109th floor of the Astrogold Tower, Max Ashman strode across to the full length mirror on the wall of his office. He looked at this reflection critically, smoothed his gray-streaked blond hair, and brushed a minute fleck from his sleeve. Restlessly, he went across to the window and looked down over the city, carefully controlling his breathing rhythm for a minute before returning to his desk.

He was irritated by the fact that he still felt a trifle apprehensive before each contact with the two senior directors. Perhaps it was because he was aware of their immense age, with its accumulated reservoir of experience. They were the last of a small group of people who had formed the Astrogold Corporation nearly a century ago.

The muted chime of a bell brought his attention to an area of empty space on the side of his office away from the windows. The outside view darkened to the semblance of night as the windows became opaque, and

11

simultaneously with the change in polarization a floor-to-ceiling hologram cube brightened. It looked like a doorway opening into another room, with a sloping stretch of beach beyond its open door stretching down to an emerald lagoon. A spray-showered reef, possibly artificial, divided the lagoon from dark blue water beyond.

Garth DiMauro's image strode in through the doorway, coming to a halt precisely in the center of the hologram cube, so realistic that a stranger entering the office would have immediately accepted the fact that he was simply standing there in the room. The last of Astrogold's founding directors, he was a hundred and thirty-seven years old. Much of his body was metal and plastic and printed circuitry and intricate hydraulic systems—exactly how much, only his doctors knew—but his brain was still coldly alert. He looked at Ashman with calm, observant eyes, the irises of which were now almost colorless. His skin was the color of old ivory, his hair completely white, his mouth a straight slit above an outthrust chin.

"What's the problem, Max?" His voice had a metallic sound.

"Anton Slade. You remember him?"

The suggestion that DiMauro might not have remembered was a tactical error, Ashman realized as soon as he had said it. The ancient, gray-white eyes flashed.

"Of course I remember him. One of our star products of the Institute. Handling our operations out on Ceres."

Ashman nodded. "He *was* running our Ceres center. Now, he seems to have disappeared."

DiMauro's eyes widened momentarily, then narrowed. "Disappeared? An accident?"

Ashman shook his head. "I don't think so. He's severed all connection with the Corporation."

"When?"

"Officially, I've just learned of it. But there was some sign of a break coming a few months ago."

"Why wasn't I informed then?"

"It seemed indefinite at first, and I put it down to the normal, periodic discontent of a man spending a long time out in the Belt."

"I should have been told straight away." DiMauro's eyes were like steel. "Anything involving an Institute man is on a different order of magnitude from a matter concerning our general personnel. You people represent an investment—our guarantee for the future—our expansion into a new frontier." He flung his arms outward and upward in a flamboyant gesture. "A frontier more exciting than outer space itself."

The single note of the bell interrupted him, and the two of them turned towards a second hologram cube shining close to an adjacent wall of the office, giving a view of a large room with bookshelves like a public library. In front of the shelving, a thin woman with blue-white skin sat in a small electric car, one transparent, almost skeletal hand arranging her white hair. Ashman bowed slightly.

"Good to see you looking so well, Mac," he said. "Garth and I were just discussing—"

"I heard it," she snapped in a brittle voice. Almost a century ago, when Garth DiMauro had been the youngest of the founding directors of Astrogold, Lakshmi McLaren had been his private secretary. A few decades later, when time had depleted the ranks of the original group, she had been made an associate director, and today she and DiMauro were nominally the co-rulers of the corporation's empire. Unlike DiMauro, who liked to advertise his hundred and thirty-seven years of accumulated experience and wisdom, she never stated her age, but there would have been little difference in their years. "I agree with Garth," she said. "We should have been told of this."

She looked up at Ashman with the same direct stare as DiMauro. One of her eyes was the same faded, gray-white color as DiMauro's, the other a warm brown. The brown one was obviously a transplant, but she never revealed who the donor had been, nor under what circumstances the transplant had been made.

Ashman took a deep, long breath before answering. He looked from one to the other of the two images. "Over the last few years, you've given me a very free hand in the running of the corporation. Obviously, you've found my judgement satisfactory. Here, I think I can keep up the standard. I know Anton Slade. Knew him from boyhood, from the Prometheus Institute days. He's brilliant, by anyone's measure."

"We're aware of that," said DiMauro.

"Of course. No question of that. But out on Ceres, he's been working in a relatively primitive environment, among people less—less complicated than he is. I believe he's developed temporary delusions of grandeur." He managed a cool smile. "But I've already taken steps to handle the situation."

Their responses were fired at him simultaneously. "What steps?" "What have you done?"

"I'm going to send Kingston Hannan out there to straighten things out.".

"King Hannan?" DiMauro tilted his head back, thrusting out his chin. "But that means doing without Hannan for a year!"

"I think the situation justifies it. You see, Slade has been unhappy about the winding down of our gold mining operations. Against a head office directive, he sent a consignment of gold that would be enough to finally wreck the international market. Admittedly, he's produced it more cheaply than ever before. You'll remember, of course, that he initiated what he called Project Aura. He found an asteroid of almost solid gold, a kilometer in diameter, some years ago. He built rockets into it and actually moved it into an orbit around Ceres, then sent the gold down in magnetic launchers to the surface of Ceres for processing and re-shipment."

DiMauro and McLaren looked at Ashman for a few seconds without speaking. Then DiMauro said: "That's not the whole story, is it, Max?"

The violet light glowed on Ashman's intercom. He reached for it. "Yes?"

Jaya's face appeared in the cube. "King Hannan's arrived."

"Tell him to wait out there for a minute." Ashman snapped off the intercom, then looked straight at DiMauro. "All right. It's *not* the whole story. I don't know whether you've heard it independently, but Slade made a threat. A threat to the whole corporation. I didn't take it seriously at first, but now it appears that Slade is in sympathy with the colonists who want self-government out there."

"That's understandable," put in Lakshmi McLaren unexpectedly. "Some of them are second and third generation roiders. They've grown up in almost zero gravity, and they wouldn't be able to adapt to living anywhere else. But that doesn't apply to Slade."

"He seems to feel that we gave him a bad deal. He also feels that Earth as a whole gave Ceres and the other roids a poor deal."

"But what was this threat he made?" asked DiMauro. "What could he possibly do to Earth?"

"As to that, I've been trying to think like Slade. Now look at this! One of his major achievements was moving an asteroid from its orbit. A metallic asteroid three kilometers in diameter. Now if he's done that once, he can do it again."

"But the asteroids are a very long way from here," said Mac.

Ashman turned towards her. "How about the Amor type roids. The ones they used to call the Earth-grazers. A stupid name, I know, because the closest of them misses us by nearly a million kilometers. However, Slade's technique of nudging one from its orbit could make it awkward for us."

There was a heavy silence. When the others did not speak, Ashman went on.

"Remember, there's a theory that an asteroid strike wiped out the dinosaurs all over the Earth—probably a roid only five or six kilometers in diameter."

"You think Slade would actually *do* that?" DiMauro's voice shook.

"I think it should be checked out. After all, I think he's capable of working out the technique in very accurate detail."

"But they'd pick it up on radar," objected Mac.

DiMauro turned quickly towards her. "Not necessarily in time." He turned back to Ashman. "King Hannan, now. Do you think he could handle the situation?"

"He's had plenty of space experience, although he's never been out to the roids. Incidentally, I believe he's on the verge of a break-up with his girl. That should put him in a suitable attitude of mind to act as a hatchet man, if necessary." He gestured towards the outer room. "He's waiting out there at the moment. You want to be in on the interview?"

The two images in the holograms exchanged glances. Although all three people at the interview were hundreds of kilometers apart, the cameras and projectors were placed so that in each of the three locations the scene was the same, except that it was Ashman who was merely a speaking light-image in the others.

"You handle it," said DiMauro. "We'll be here, but we'll be off visual. If we want to come in, we'll give you the bell, then you can give us the usual greeting."

A touch on their hand-held-remote control units, and the lighted cubes of the holograms vanished. The outer windows re-polarized to allow the full blaze of sunlight into the office, and Ashman immediately reached for his intercom.

A door slid open in the dark blue wall, and King Hannan strode in. They had known each other long enough for their greeting to be limited to a nod, a grin and a raised eyebrow. Ashman touched a control, and a magnagrav chair slid from its recess and floated in front of his desk. King sat down on it and leaned back.

"Good to be back with the joys of civilization," he said. "This must be something really big, Max. What is it? End of the world?"

Ashman didn't smile. "I wouldn't joke about a thing like that, King."

King's smile faded as they sat looking at each other. After a few seconds, he spread out his hands. "Perhaps you'd better fill me in."

"Right," said Ashman, but for a few moments he said nothing, looking down at his hands, which he was resting palm-down on his desk. He seemed to be having trouble selecting a starting point. Abruptly, he looked up.

"We're having a bit of trouble with Anton Slade," he said.

"Anton? That figures, Max. Always the individualist —a light-year ahead of the human race, the way he saw it."

"I know. Essentially a loner, although he had the knack of influencing people when he wanted to. That's why we gave him the Ceres project to set up."

King rubbed his chin with his fingertips. "I understood he did a tremendous job out there."

"Oh, he did. He did! Better than anyone had anticipated. He not only revolutionized our mining methods out on the roids, he was elected mayor of Piazzi City after he'd been out there only a couple of years—that's the biggest city out in the Belt. When he retired as mayor one of their years later—that's about 4.6 of our years—some of the local people made a serious suggestion that the place should have been renamed Slade City. After all, they said, Piazzi—the astronomer who discovered Ceres—had been dead for hundreds of years, and they like to look forward, not back."

"What did he do that made such an impression on them?"

"For one thing, he made Ceres self-sufficient. As a spare time activity, he started a firm called Nitro Titan. Heard of it?"

"Not that I recall."

"They bring nitrogen to some of the major roids from Titan, the big moon of Saturn. That means they can grow their own vegetation. Crops, you name it. They used to get their nitrogen from Earth, like almost everything else. Now, they can do without our help, and I think it's gone to their heads."

"Anton must have been out there quite a long time, if it's been three of their years. Two years, you said, then mayor for a year? Multiplied by four point six—"

"I can tell you his total time there. More than fourteen of our years. He came back once to take his girl out there. Gail something-or-other, you might remember her. Anyway, she couldn't stand the life there, and eventually she came back. That was a couple of years ago. Our years, I mean."

"How did he take it?"

"Not very well, I think. That's when he first started to ignore our directives. The last shipment of gold was the final cruncher."

"What was that?"

"Oh, forgot you'd been away for a while. Gold prices have dropped over the last years. Graph's gone down like a waterfall. We told Slade no more gold for a while, concentrate on other metals. Trouble was, he'd just moved an almost solid gold asteroid to a close orbit around Ceres. Sent us a shipload. Thought it would pay for all the improvements Ceres needed. Now, he doesn't answer our communications."

"Perhaps he's dead."

Ashman shook his head. "We got some outside information on him, but it's sketchy. When the Ceres people started agitating for self-government a while back, Anton was on their side. He even made a threat. Said he thought the asteroids represented the advancing edge of human civilization, that we were the moribund core of it, not nearly as secure as we believed."

"Sounds a pretty empty threat to me. Maybe it was a case of drink talking."

"I don't think so. Certainly not empty. This fellow can move asteroids from their orbit."

King felt suddenly cold. "I've read horror articles about asteroid strikes. The Canyon Diablo in America. The Hennebery Craters and Gosse's Bluff. And the thing that wiped out the era of the dinosaurs. But, hell, that was sixty million years ago, wasn't it?"

Ashman's reply was in a low, thoughtful tone. "Sixty-three million, to be more exact. I've been doing some checking."

"Got you worried enough for that, has it?"

Ashman shrugged. "May be nothing in it. On the other hand, if there's any chance at all that Slade may launch an attack on us with a controlled asteroid or meteor impact, we'd better find out about it before it happens."

"Wouldn't this be a job for the Peacekeeping Force?"

"Bunch of raw amateurs in this field, King. Now *you* know Anton Slade as well as anyone. I want you to go out to Ceres and contact him."

"God, wouldn't it take me a year to get there?"

"Not now. We've got it down to a matter of months."

"And you want me to go out there *alone*—remember, I've never been out to Ceres—and try to track down a man who's been in the roids for fourteen years?"

"You have the authority to co-opt anyone out there who might be able to help. You know, local knowledge, specialist techniques, and so on."

"When do you want me to leave?"

"There's a transport in Earth orbit right now, due to leave when it finishes loading in about three days. I can get you up to it on one of the shuttles the day after tomorrow."

"I want to see Moya before I go."

"Sure. Take her out on the town tonight. I'll pick up all your bills."

King nodded thoughtfully. "And I'd like to do something else."

"What's that?"

"I'd like to see Slade's woman."

"What good would that do?"

"She probably has a better idea how he's thinking right now than anyone else. After all, she was with him until a couple of years ago. You've only had messages from—what is it?—best part of three hundred million kilometers away. An edited message over that distance tells you just what the fellow wants you to hear, but it tells you nothing about the way he *feels*. What did you say her name was? Gail—?"

"Hold it." Ashman reached for his intercom. In the shining surface of the Astrogold logo on the wall behind him, King could see a tiny reflection of the hologram cube within its hood. Jaya's face appeared, recognizable in spite of the distorted reflection.

"Jaya," said Ashman. "Find the name of Anton Slade's lady, and where to contact her."

Looking up again at King, he said: "I'll give you all the data on the Ceres office before you lift off. Slade had only local people on his staff. A woman called Silvi was his secretary, so she might be a point of contact when you get there. There are only about a hundred thousand people in Piazzi City."

"As many as that?"

"A lot of it's underground. Some of it in domes."

The intercom cube lit up again, and Jaya's face appeared. "Here's the data on Gail Busuttil."

"Right," said Ashman. A series of words filled the screen, and he pressed a button to take a hard copy. He ran off two copies of the material on the screen, and passed one of them to King, who glanced at it.

"Not far away," he said. "I'll look her up, after I've straightened things out with Moya."

Ashman leaned back in his chair. "Like to contact the two senior directors?"

King looked up in some surprise. "If you think so."

"You *are* going away on a long journey, and you'll be spending a lot of corporation money. Perhaps it would be as well."

"As you wish, Max. You have more contact with them than I do."

Ashman turned to his intercom and reached out to it. "Jaya," he said. "Would you see if you could raise the two senior directors? Thanks." And he appeared to switch off the intercom again. Looking at the reflection in the gold emblem behind him, King noticed that this time there was no image of Jaya in the small hooded hologram cube. He studied Ashman's face intently while Ashman was looking away from him.

A few seconds later, a bell sounded, and one of the large cubes lit up, the windows darkening. Garth DiMauro's image stood there.

"Garth," said Ashman, "I'd like you to meet Kingston Hannan again."

"Call me Garth," said DiMauro. "I remember you well, Kingston. The Prometheus Institute, right?" At this moment the other cube lit up, and DiMauro turned. "You've met Lakshmi McLaren, of course."

"Call me Mac," said the woman, looking up at King with her non-matching eyes.

"I've already told you of our problem with Anton Slade," said Ashman. "King's going to go out to Ceres to contact him."

DiMauro's eyes swept King. Eyes that looked as if they had seen everything that human eyes could see. "Excellent!" he said. "Keeping it in the family, eh? Any problem an Institute man is involved in can only be settled by another Institute man, right?"

"Right," said Ashman.

DiMauro looked piercingly at King. "We have great faith in you people, son. As I've often said, with our hormonal engineering techniques at the Institute we're opening up a new frontier."

The woman gave a dry little laugh. "Judging from our experience with Slade, it may be a dark frontier."

DiMauro gave no sign of having heard her. He kept looking fixedly at King as if he were trying to hypnotize him. "Whatever you need to do, remember we're behind you. Max will arrange for you to use the money we have out in Piazzi City."

The interview finished quickly, leaving King with the vague feeling that something was wrong, something that he would have recognized had he been more relaxed.

"Well," said Ashman. "Looks as if it's fixed."

"I'll have a lot of things to tie up in the next day or two," said King. "Can you let me have a vehicle?"

"Check with Jaya on the way out. She has the keys of the pool cars."

"Right."

It was only when he was riding down in the elevator that King fitted it together. That second call on the intercom that Ashman had made—the one that did not show Jaya's image on the cube reflected in the golden wall-emblem. Ashman had not really made the call at all. Yet DiMauro and Mac had appeared shortly afterwards, without having any call passed on to them by Jaya. They could not have timed their appearance so precisely in advance. They had obviously been listening to the entire interview between him and Ashman with the visual turned off. He felt sudden, cold anger. The thought came to him momentarily that if the corporation functioned like that, perhaps Anton Slade was right.

THREE

The aircar they had reserved for King was a late model, colored an unobtrusive brown, with good air conditioning. The Astrogold emblem on the door was small and restrained. He took off, joined one of the traffic lanes marked out by filmy vertical planes of tinted light, and headed towards the suburb called Arcturus Lake.

In spite of the mushroom crop of new structures, he easily picked out the residential building where Moya lived, a sixty-story tower of jade-green glassite. Her apartment was on the thirty-third floor, just three levels above the restaurant complex, and he landed on the flange marked "30" and rode the escalators up three floors.

Room 3314. He stopped in front of her jade plastic door and pressed his hand against the palm-plate. He heard the bell chime within, the door slid open and her voice said "Come in, King." It was a recording, but at least she had left him on the list of intimates stored in her computer.

"Are you there, Moya?" he called as he walked through the living room.

Her reply came in a recording activated by the sound of his voice: "I'll be back around thirteen thirty, King. You know where the drinks are. Enjoy my view while you wait. Oh, there's a new cassette on the little malachite table."

He looked at his watch. She'd be back in ten minutes. He walked across to one of the outer windows and looked down over the lake, where a hovercraft loaded with vacationers skimmed across the surface like a giant version of a pond-skating insect.

Just a minute short of thirteen thirty, Moya's little emerald-green aircar swung down on to the flange at level 30. She stepped out of it, her supple, bronzed limbs a shade longer than he had remembered them, in a small, sleeveless wrap-around. Since he had seen her on the video she had changed her hair from red to orange. She took a couple of parcels from the car, and hurried across to the escalators.

He met her just inside the front door of her flat, only giving her time to put her parcels down before embracing her. After the first kiss, she held her head back.

"How do you like me tall?"

Her large green eyes were now almost on a level with his. He scanned her face, the outlining of her eyes, the lifted eyebrow, the quirk of the opposite corner of her maroon-outlined mouth, the slightly shortened nose.

"I like," he said emphatically. "More accessible." He demonstrated with a more prolonged kiss, his hands massaging her lean, muscular back.

"You're not going back into space again, I hope," she said.

"I'm going to need to use some diplomacy about that. I'm having a session with Ashman tomorrow. He wants me to make another trip, but I'll see what I can do."

He felt her stiffen slightly in his embrace. "Where does he want you to go?" she asked.

"Listen, I wouldn't worry about it right now, Moya. It mightn't happen."

"Something tells me it will."

He shook her gently. "Leave it to me. I'm working on it. Now, what have you been doing?"

She leaned back, one hand clasping the other wrist behind his neck. "Bought a new dress just now."

"Let's see it."

Stepping back from him, she tossed off the green wrap-around, standing perfectly naked except for her shoes. She slipped a filmy, rainbow-tinted garment on, pulling it tightly around her body and pressing it shut with her hand.

"Good," he said, "but wrong hair."

She went to a dressing table, slid open a drawer, and held up two wigs, one black, one chestnut, questioning with her eyes.

"The black," he said.

She stripped off the orange wig and tossed it on to the dressing table, and ran her hand over the brown stubble of hair covering her scalp. She took a cordless electric shaver from the table and began sweeping it backwards and forwards over her head.

"Where would you like us to go this evening?" asked King, raising his voice to compete with the hum of the razor close to her ear.

She turned to the mirror as she shaved. "There's a new light-show at the Orinoco. Their meals are quite good, and so's the music. I want to see if we dance better now we're nearer the same height. There." She put on the black, short-cropped wig, adjusted it, then turned for King's evaluation.

"Tremendous!" he said. "Say I pick you up about twenty hundred?"

"What are you doing this afternoon?"

"Trying to trace an old friend of mine from the Prometheus Institute. Fellow called Anton Slade."

"Didn't he go out to some appalling place in the asteroids?"

"Yes. I believe he did. Not sure where he is now." He shrugged. "Anyway, I'm going to try to trace him through a woman friend of his who still lives around this way. Woman called Gail Busuttil."

Moya frowned slightly. "I think I may have met her at Gazelles. All the really forward-looking girls have been going there this year. Does she run some kind of consultant business?"

"That sounds like her."

"Don't know what people consult her about—but I think she'd be very bright. She's one of those Santoro women, you know?"

He shook his head. "Santoro?"

"Oh, the Santoro Technique is that one where they take a bright girl in her teens and graft a whole lot of cultured brain cortex tissue into her. They make her a high artificial skull of hard plastic, and build some kind of in-body computer into her. One day at Gazelles she played twenty of us at chess simultaneously and beat all of us."

"And that's Gail Busuttil? Could be the same—Anton Slade took her out to Ceres with him when he first went there. I never met her, although I knew him." He looked at his watch. "Well, Moya—at twenty hundred. Do I have to book at the Orinoco?"

"I'll do that, if you have a lot on your program."

Flying westward, King slipped his small note-terminal from his pocket and quickly tapped a few keys. He read the address that appeared on its miniscule screen, then looked down to identify the building where Gail Busuttil lived. He found it in a line of tall structures of mixed business and residential classification, along a curve of artificial hills overlooking the Torrens Seaway.

The address on the terminal led him to a tower of green-gold metal and ruby glassite. He landed on a flange at level 25, and only one floor above he saw a discreet sign above a line of windows: G. Busuttil—Consultant.

He rode the escalator up and pressed the buzzer outside a ruby door bearing a smaller version of the same sign. Through a speaker beside the door a woman's voice said "Busuttil."

King spoke into the microphone. "My name is King Hannan. I was a friend of Anton Slade. I'm trying to get in touch with him, and I thought you might be able to help."

"I haven't seen him for two years." Her voice was well modulated and carefully controlled.

"I knew him at the Prometheus Institute," said King. Looking upward, he saw the lens of a camera surveying him.

"Come in," said the woman, and the ruby door slid open.

King walked in along a green-walled passage. Another door was open at one side of it, and he went through into a living room as the outer door closed behind him. The room had deep wall-to-wall carpeting, and several magnagrav chairs and a table floated here and there.

A tall, slim woman in a red, glossy tunic stood facing him. She had lightly tanned skin, and she was completely hairless, with slender eyebrows tattooed high above her large, dark eyes, giving her a permanent expression of bored surprise. Involuntarily King found his eyes straying to the unnaturally high, bald dome of her head, and he quickly brought his gaze down to meet her direct stare.

"Why did you think I could help you to find Anton?" she asked in a level voice.

"I understand you lived with him for a number of years."

"Twelve years. I left him two years ago."

"I'm sorry to hear that," said King.

"Why?" She smiled slightly. "It was a mutual decision—suited both of us."

For once, King was not quite sure what to say. She moved a little closer to him, her eyes never leaving his. "King—may I call you King?—people come to me with all kinds of problems. Often, the one they mention first isn't anywhere near the heart of their difficulty. We're obviously both busy people. Why not save our time and come straight to your main focus?"

King hesitated, then shrugged. He gave a tired grin. "I'm sorry. The fact is, Anton Slade made some kind of threat to the Corporation."

The dark eyes suddenly narrowed and brightened. "A threat?" Abruptly, she indicated one of the floating magnagrav chairs. "This may take a little time, then. Would you like something to drink?"

"Thanks. I'll leave it to you."

As he sat down, she turned and strode briskly across to a complex drink-dispenser against one wall. It was the first time he had been able to study her. She was a trim, well co-ordinated woman, slim except for the startlingly prominent breasts thrusting out against her red tunic. Now that she was standing with her side to him, he saw that she had a rounded hump across the back of her shoulders, so that the upper part of her body was disproportionately deep from front to back. He remembered what Moya had said about the built-in computer. The high, ovoid, hairless head was set directly on her shoulders without an intervening neck.

Turning, she brought two tall glasses of clear liquid across, handing one to King and sitting opposite him with the other. She lifted her glass, which had a bent glass straw.

"To Anton, the way we remember him," she said.

"To Anton," agreed King, "whatever he's doing."

They each drank a little. King found that he began to feel more relaxed.

"Now," said the woman. "What was this threat?"

"I didn't hear it directly. But Max Ashman—that's our Managing Director—is worried by the fact that Anton had developed a technique for moving asteroids."

"And you think he may use one as a weapon?"

"Perhaps."

"But what target?"

At this instant the chime of a bell interrupted her, and she rose and walked up to one end of the room, standing facing a blank wall. She touched a control on a broad, ornamental bangle on her left wrist, and the wall became a 3D screen showing two men and a woman sitting at a desk cluttered with diagrams and computer printouts.

"Busuttil," said one of the men. "We've run into a problem." There followed an intricate discussion, the three people on the screen sometimes speaking all at once. King was astounded at the ease and speed with which Gail apparently solved a difficulty that he could not even comprehend. She used a display screen at one side, tapping the complex keyboard in front of it, filling it with swarms of shining figures that often persisted for only a fraction of a second.

"It can be done," she said, and the trio on the screen listened to her intently. "Trouble's induced magnetic field. If the foam steel of the body is at least 13 per cent manganese, it will be non-magnetic. Ashikaga will be able to do that for you. Give them the dimensions today, they'll shuttle it down tomorrow."

"Could you rough us out a diagram?" asked one of the men.

Without speaking, she cleared the display terminal and began drawing an extremely complex pattern with a light-pen. When she had finished, she stepped aside. "Copy okay?" she asked.

"Thanks, Busuttil," said the man who had spoken.

"We'd be lost without you, Busuttil," said the woman on the screen.

Gail gave them a brilliant smile, and the picture vanished. At once, she strode back to the seat opposite King, sitting down and resuming her conversation as if there had been no interruption of any kind.

"What target?" she asked.

"Eh?"

She looked slightly impatient. "You said Anton might be tempted to use an asteroid off-orbit as a weapon. Against what?"

"We have no idea. Perhaps Earth. Could he do that?"

For the first time, she looked a little shaken. Her eyes widened and darkened, and she rolled them aside as if lost in private thoughts for a few seconds. Then she looked back at King.

"Perhaps I should explain why Anton and I went

separate ways," she said. "He believed the asteroid culture represented the cutting edge of civilization, as he called it. He did a lot to begin the present view, current in the roids, that the Earth is decadent. It's true, from an engineering and astronautical viewpoint, Out There is where it's all happening. But life has other aspects."

She took a sip of her drink, the long, bent straw between her lips. The light tan plastic that formed the artificial skull seemed to be fused at the edges with her skin. King suddenly realised another thing that was strange about her. She had no external ears—just little grilles shielding membranes at each side of her head.

"How did you first meet?" asked King.

"He took a crash course in history before he went out to the roids, and I was his tutor. He was the brightest star in my class, and I was the first woman he'd met with computer-enhanced recall. We made a good team out on Ceres." She smiled wryly. "I probably implanted in him the idea that civilization spreads out from its original foci, with the most advanced achievements out along the periphery rather than at the core. I used instances from Earth history, he extrapolated into space development."

"I think there's a lot of truth in that."

"Of course there is, but it's only one side of the truth, one facet. Anton began ordering his life as if he'd never return to Earth. But two or three years ago I realized I'd be better employed back here. I had a responsibility."

"Yes?" prompted King.

She lifted her hands and slid them up over the high plastic dome. "This cost millions. It's like the hormonal engineering that you and Anton have had. I wasn't being used to full capacity out there." She was silent for nearly half a minute. Then her expression changed. "What action are you taking about this threat of Anton's?"

"Astrogold is sending me out there to find out what he's doing. After all, I know him better than any of them."

"When are you going?"

"There's a Ceres ship in Earth orbit now. They're shuttling me up the day after tomorrow."

"Have you had much experience in space?"

"Just had three months at L5. Last year, the Moon."

"The roid settlements can be varied, some of them very primitive. Still, you should survive. Anton and I did." She stood up, her hands in the front pockets of her tunic, looking down at him over her prominent breasts.

King stood up. "Well, you've filled in the picture of Anton quite a bit. Thanks, Gail—if I may call you Gail."

Her eyes looked directly into his. "Do you want to develop a sexual relationship with me?"

"No. At least—no."

Her expression was unreadable. "Most people simply call me Busuttil."

He bowed slightly. "Well, thanks, Busuttil."

He went out to his aircar. As he was lifting off, he glanced up at her window. She was standing looking down at him, hands still resting in the pockets of her tunic. When he waved to her she seemed to ignore the gesture for a second or two, then she lifted her hand in a quick answering wave.

The Orinoco was built on a peninsula running out into the lake. Energy fields controlled the air above it, retaining a micro-climate that filled its surroundings with damp tropical jungle, but the tables were set on a large, free-form staging always swept by a cool, simulated sea breeze.

"Had a busy time since you left me?" asked Moya.

King nodded. "First, a session with Slade's woman to see what else I could find out about him. Then the library, to brush up on some data about asteroid orbits. Then another short session with Max Ashman. It's a wild life, isn't it?"

Moya, looking upward, gave a shrill cry of delight as a shower of liquid light curved above them, changing in seconds from cerise to lime green to azure. King looked

at the line of her slim, smooth throat as she tilted her
head back. Her small earrings sparkled in the changing
light. She caught him watching her and smiled.

"You were right about my hair. Black goes with any
of these colors."

He nodded. "Push it back at the sides to show your
ears. You have lovely ears."

"Thanks. But perhaps that's only because you've
been with Domehead."

"Who?"

She laughed as she picked up a sumosa and began to
eat. "Gail Busuttil. We used to call her Domehead at
Gazelles. She's bright, though. Nearly finished up running the place. Better watch her, though. She can get
any man she wants—which just shows you how much
the beauticians know. Looks as if hair and ears have
nothing to do with sex attraction."

"She seemed aloof to me."

"Likes men younger than herself, I think. Thing is,
she remembers everything about a man—everything he
likes, whatever interests him, what turns him on—it all
goes into that computer she has inside her. Anyway, did
you tell Ashman you're not going into space again?"

He hesitated. She froze, a sumosa half lifted to her
mouth. Slowly, she put it down.

"You're *not* going back out there, are you?"

He nodded. "I can't get out of it. I have to go out to
Ceres."

"Ceres! God, that's right out on the far side of the
asteroids, isn't it?"

"Yes." He looked at her for a few seconds and came
to a decision. "Want to come with me? I could swing it
with Astrogold."

"King, that has to be a joke. From what I hear, Ceres
is nothingsville."

"It's growing. It's exciting to see a place that's
developing."

"It can develop without me!" She looked at him with
an explosive blaze of anger, sitting straight up, her meal
forgotten. "Don't bother to look for me after you come

back. *If* you come back. I'm not something you can plug in and switch on whenever you feel—" Her voice broke, and she quickly turned to look away over the lake.

He reached over and put his hand on her arm, but she pulled it sharply away. Suddenly she stood up, pulling her cloak around her shoulders and fastening the emerald clasp at her throat.

"Take me home, King," she said in a quiet voice.

In this eruption of moods, there was no point in arguing. He drove her to her apartment, and she went quickly inside without inviting him to follow. He walked slowly back to his aircar.

"Damn Ceres," he said aloud. "And damn Max." The target of his fury kept shifting, until finally it came into focus.

"Above all, damn Anton Slade!"

FOUR

Seen from the shuttle, the freighter *Karl Friedrich Gauss* was enormous, the largest mobile structure King had seen. It was a metal cylinder well over a thousand meters long and a hundred in diameter. Its hull was made of foamed nickel-manganese steel that had been produced in zero gravity, its thickness giving good meteoroid protection without adding too much mass.

There were three other passengers in the shuttle, together with many tons of freight. King had not seen his fellow travellers yet except as anonymous figures in space-suits—a company regulation required that suits be worn in boarding any interplanetary craft.

The *Gauss* was spinning slowly on its long axis to create artificial gravity on its cylindrical inside "floor." The shuttle took up a position astern, matched spin, and moved slowly within, docking virtually on the axis, in zero gravity.

Emerging, King was astounded at the vastness of the space inside the freighter. Still in their suits, the quartet rode an elevator down to "floor" level, weight gradually coming to them as they sank lower. Weighing nearly 80 kilograms plus a roughly equal weight for his suit, King stepped out into a kilometer-long passageway that seemed to extend forward almost to infinity, lit by cool fluorescent tubes.

A lean, red-haired young man with freckles and an infectious grin met them, and gestured towards a changing room where they were able to get out of their suits in small cubicles, leaving each suit under a hand-lettered card bearing the owner's name.

"I'm the Second Officer, Red Parkes," he said. "Call me Red—everyone does. You, I take it, would be Kingston Hannan?" King nodded, and the man turned to the others. "And you'd be the Ferris family. John, Margaret and daughter Elsa."

"Correct," said the man in a loud, ringing voice. He was of medium height, but looked somehow taller, gray haired, with a gray beard, about sixty. He wore an old-fashioned gray suit and old-style glasses. His wife was plump, gray, also in glasses of out-of-date styling, obviously a woman dedicated to keeping a low profile.

The daughter was quite different, blonde, tanned, an outdoor girl with clear blue eyes. At first glance, about seventeen. On closer inspection, somewhere in her mid-twenties. Altogether, they seemed a most unlikely trio to be making a voyage out to Ceres.

The ship carried only a small number of passengers, most of its inside space being reserved for bulk freight or containers.

"Any more of us?" King asked Red.

"One more shuttle to come up. Might be someone on that."

King found his cabin small but well designed. He unpacked a load of printouts filled with data on Ceres and the other main asteroids. Ceres was larger than he had thought, nearly eight hundred kilometers in diameter. There were uncounted thousands of asteroids, but the largest three, Ceres, Pallas and Vesta, contained more than half the total matter of the Belt.

At the orbit of Ceres, the Belt measured nearly thirteen hundred million kilometers around, and it was millions of kilometers wide. That was a vast amount of space in which to search for Anton Slade.

King met the Ferris family shortly afterwards in the canteen, where Red had suggested coffee. John Ferris talked in reverberating clichés, like an old-style preacher who had lost all belief in what he was saying, but kept on because it was expected of him.

"We ran an Alternative Society in the South Pacific," he said. Somehow, he seemed to use capital letters in his speech. "We believe that mankind has taken a wrong road, and that the best guarantee of survival is by living in a completely natural way."

"That depends on how far you go back," said King.

"What do you mean?" asked Ferris.

"It could mean getting your meal by chasing it and choking it."

The girl turned away as a spontaneous laugh bubbled up in her. Her mother glared at her. Her father opened his mouth, closed it again and turned his attention to his coffee.

It looked like a dull voyage as far as companionship was concerned, thought King. He tried to rectify the damage he seemed to have done to the Ferris self-esteem.

"Is your society still operating?" he asked.

Ferris shook his head. "Alas, no. The young members tend to drift away. Last year, a hurricane wrecked what was left of our entire project."

"I'm sorry," said King. "I take it you've sold up and are starting again out in the asteroids."

"Something like that," said Ferris, and he got up as if to stop the conversation developing any further. "Come, Mother," he said, and his wife rose at once. "Elsa?"

"I think I'll have another coffee, Dad," she said. Her parents went out.

King glanced after them. "Hope I didn't say something wrong,'' he said to the girl.

She thrust out her lower lip. "I think you did, but it doesn't matter. Dad isn't used to being questioned."

She sipped her coffee, and he looked at her curiously. She wore no makeup, yet she looked freshly attractive. "It's quite a big step to go out to a place like Ceres. Have you any contacts there?"

"Yes, my elder sister, Yetta. She lives out there with her man. They prospect small asteroids for metals, and lately they've made quite a lot of money. Yetta's paying our fares out."

"That's generous of her."

"It's more complicated than that. You see, my parents have always believed in living a natural life. No medical interference with the course of nature, and all the rest of it. But Yetta's a dwarf. What they call an achondroplasic—very short arms and legs. That can be treated now—could have been treated then!—but Dad didn't believe in medical help of any kind. As a result—" She held out her hand, palm-down, about the level of the table. "Yetta's only that high. Of course, she didn't fit in with Dad's nature theories, and when she was twenty-one she took her share of the family fortune and bought herself a ticket to Ceres. I'm afraid she left us as a very angry little lady."

"Well, you may find things are sorting themselves out."

The girl shook her head. "I think my parents are naive, in a way. They don't realize Yetta can be a little monster."

The final shuttle came up about four hours later, but King did not see it arrive, as he was seeing Captain East with the object of having himself placed in cryptobiosis as soon as possible after the ship went into ion drive. He had no intention of wasting any more than he could help of the six months the voyage would consume.

East was a fat, blond man of about fifty. He didn't look physically fit by Earth standards, but under low gravity he probably functioned quite efficiently.

"Right," he said. "We'll put you under just after we go into the drive, and bring you out again about three days before we reach Ceres orbit. Make it closer if you like, but I wouldn't advise it."

"I'll leave it to you," said King.

When King was brought out of cryptobiosis, the gravity of the ship had been reduced to Ceres normal. When he stood up, he found that his weight was less than three kilograms. Red, used to assisting people to make the change, held his arm as he became familiar with his altered weight.

"Notice we have air bags all over the ceiling of this room," said Red. "First thing some people do, they jump up and ram their heads into the ceiling."

"I've had a bit of experience of weak gravity—never one as light as this." King gestured. "I know, we were weightless in the shuttle on the way up, but in that case we were strapped in."

"Come along to the canteen. I'll come with you, in case you forget and take a high jump."

In the canteen, King noticed four abandoned chessboards on one of the long tables. "Who plays?" he asked.

"Oh, the skipper and the engineer play every day, every trip. They both think they're quite good. Then this Ferris character used to play with them—he doesn't believe in cryptobio, so the three of them used to play, and sometimes I'd come in. Then this other passenger— the woman who came up on the last shuttle—she took the whole four of us on at a simultaneous game, and cleaned up the lot of us. Didn't even seem to take time to think between her moves. I think it took a couple of years off the skipper's life! Ferris, too."

"Who is she?"

"Oh, she's a domehead. You know—" He held his hand about a hand-span above his scalp. "Plastic skull right up like this, hump on her back with a computer in it."

"What's her name?"

"Busuttil. Bloody interesting woman to talk to. Seems to know about everything. Big opinion of herself, but I suppose that's justified."

"I'd like to meet her."

"I think she went up the forward observation room. You can ride the trolley along."

King rode the swift-moving little electric trolley along the passageway to the bow of the ship, with its heavy glassite windows. She was not there, but he found the engineer standing with a pair of binoculars. Hearing King come up behind him, he turned.

"You can just make out Ceres. There, near the Scorpion. See, the big red one's Antares, and the white's Shaula. Ceres is the slightly yellowish one between them. With the glasses, you can see it as a disc."

"Was Gail Busuttil up here?"

"The bald woman? Went back to her cabin, I think. She flattened the skipper and me at chess, and two others at the same time." The engineer was a stocky, earnest man. He turned to King again. "Why do they do a thing like that to a woman? I suppose if they gave a man that much brain, he'd try to rule the Solar System. A woman just goes around being a pain in the base to the rest of us."

"Why? Because she beat you all at chess?"

"Oh, not only that. Thinks she knows everything."

"I've met plenty of people who think like that."

"Yes. But she *does* know bloody near everything."

King gestured towards Ceres. "When do you arrive?"

The engineer looked at his watch. "About seventy hours from now we should be going into a Ceres orbit. They send up their shuttles, then—they're usually quite quick. There are only five passengers, so you'll all go down in the first trip."

"Looking forward to seeing Piazzi City."

"It's quite a place, Piazzi. But maybe I'm biased. It's my home town."

King rode the trolley back along the monotonous, dimly lit kilometer of the passageway, and parked it where he had found it, outside the canteen. As he was walking past he glanced in and saw an unmistakable figure standing at the coffee dispenser. She was wearing a long, wrap-around skirt of the same pale tan color as her skin, and a short, matching cape.

He walked quietly in behind her. "Congratulations," he said.

She whirled, the short cape swirling out. Her outstanding breasts were quite real, now that he saw them uncovered. "Congratulations? On what?"

"I believe you're the new chess champion of the ship."

"Oh, that?" She stood aside as he poured himself a coffee, and then they both sat carefully at one of the small tables. Neither was as yet fully comfortable in the .03g. Suddenly, she looked up at King with her eyes wide and blazing. "Usually, I have very good control of myself. But they annoyed me, especially Ferris. I came in when they were arranging a game between them. Ferris looked across and said to East 'I wonder if that bald-headed woman with the hump can play?' East came over to me and said 'Excuse me, do you play chess?' "

King began to smile, and her anger suddenly evaporated in an answering smile.

"So you cleaned them all up?" he prompted.

"It wasn't hard. Ferris took it badly. When I took his queen off, he sat back. 'Well,' he said, 'I've made one of my rare mistakes. I couldn't win from there.' So I turned the board around and played black—his side—and still won. I think he lost about a gallon of sweat."

"And now you feel better?"

"No. I feel I was trapped into a primitive display of vicious revenge."

"And you feel you should be above that?"

Her smile faded slowly. Her eyes darkened. They were actually steel gray, not brown as he had first thought—the darkness came from the dilated pupils, which almost covered the irises like pools of tar. "Don't *you* start to be smart with me,'' she said.

"I didn't intend it. I was just glad to find a human side to you."

"You're a typical human chauvinist," she said, and then her face changed in a lightning smile. "Well, perhaps not typical. There might be just a glow-worm flicker of hope for you."

He shrugged, and she looked at him for a long time without speaking. Then she said: "Why not ask me what you came in to find out."

"All right. I admit I didn't expect to see you on the ship. When I told you I'd be on it, you said nothing about our being on the same voyage."

"I didn't know then. I only made up my mind after thinking over what you'd said about Anton Slade and his threat to the corporation. I felt partly responsible. A very complex chain of causes and effects—there's no need to go into it all now—but I felt it was a situation partly of my making. So I decided to try to find Anton before it escalated."

King was puzzled. "But you can't just walk on to an interplanetary ship as if you're catching an aircraft to the next town! Max Ashman had to pull all sorts of strings to get me aboard this ship, even with a lot more time available."

She half-closed her eyelids for a moment. "You're making the same mistake as those stupid men with their chessboards. Underestimating the powers of a Dome-head."

"I never called you that."

"Everyone calls me that, behind my back. Actually, you should have been able to work it out. I've spent twelve Earth years on Ceres. The *Karl Gauss* was built and registered there, and East and Parkes both come from Piazzi City. My credit's good there, and they both know that. It only needed a video call, and I was on the shuttle."

King nodded. He stood up, slowly, arms outstretched for balance. "Care for another coffee?"

She suddenly widened her eyes briefly, and he realized

that was her equivalent of a nod. He filled two cups of coffee and took them back to the table.

"Busuttil," he said as he sat opposite her. "It occurs to me we both want the same thing, up to a point. We want to find Anton Slade. Perhaps we could pool our information."

She smiled. "I think the operative phrase there was 'up to a point,' don't you?" She inserted a long, curved plastic straw into her coffee and began drinking it, holding the cup between her breasts. They were firm, with large nipples. It came to King that much of her apparent self-control was perhaps an effect suggested by her inability to move her head in relation to her trunk.

"You have beautiful breasts," he said.

She went on drinking her coffee for a few seconds with no change in expression. "Courtesy of Gazelles," she said.

It seemed to him that any loss of control on her part was only a temporary phenomenon. Perhaps an isolated one.

FIVE

Their first impression of Ceres as they approached it from space was unexpected darkness—it appeared as an immense disc shutting out the light of uncounted stars. The albedo was only 0.06, less than that of the Earth's Moon, and in addition to this the great distance from the Sun meant that the intensity of sunlight reaching its surface was only about one-ninth of that falling on the Earth.

Much of the disc was as black as coal, but here and there dark gray and brown ridges and peaks formed huge, broken arcs, like the ringwalls of the Moon. There were large, flat, ebon areas like solidified seas—lava flows from some long-past volcanic activity triggered by the impact of smaller asteroids.

Three small moons orbited Ceres, one at least being unexpectedly bright. Whereas Ceres itself was an asteroid of the carbonaceous chondrite type, its small, bright companion was obviously one of the predominantly nickel-iron or otherwise metallic bodies of the type common in the inner orbits of the Belt, closer to the orbit of Mars.

"That's Aura," said Captain East, pointing it out to King. "Iron, nickel, gold, practically all of it metals. Three kilometers in diameter—but they brought it from an eccentric orbit that took it from just outside the orbit of Mars nearly all the way out to here."

"But how did they move a mass like that? It must weigh a million tonnes!"

"A million? You're joking! There's fifteen cubic kilometers there, average specific gravity about five. You could reckon that at about a tonne per cubic meter. So that lump of metal would have a mass of fifteen million tonnes." East gave a gesture of dismissal. "Given time, out here, you can move anything. They mounted atomic rockets in the body of it, controlled their firing by computer. Deflected the thing at the aphelion of its orbit, where its velocity was lowest, slowed it, drove it further out until they were able to bring it into a stable orbit around Ceres. Took years, but the firm that handled the project could afford to wait." He turned to King. "Fellow who did it used to be with your firm, Astro-gold."

"Anton Slade? Officially, he's *still* with us."

"Oh? Ah! Lot of kettles on the boil, Slade. By the way, we've got his ex-woman on board."

"I know."

East gave a short bark of laughter. "Take a fellow like Slade to handle her. Or perhaps he didn't. Eh?"

"Who knows? Anyway, are they still getting gold out of that thing?"

"Gold, and a lot of other useful metals. They send them down to the surface of Ceres by magnetic launcher. Practically an inexhaustible supply of very cheap metals."

"What about the other two moons?"

"They're smaller, but they were brought here the same way, for special deposits of minerals that were in short supply elsewhere. One has a lot of tungsten, for instance." He waved an arm towards the growing disc.

"Ceres is self-sufficient. What we don't have, we bring here from somewhere else."

"What's the legal position on ownership of these moons?"

"If they orbit Ceres, they're legally a part of Ceres. Simple as that."

King scanned the dark, pockmarked surface below—he was already thinking of it as "down"—but could see no evidence of habitation. Suddenly, however, a brilliant green light flashed three times on the surface, dimensionless, like an electric spark.

"That's the laser beacon from the Black Plains tower," said East. "That means their shuttle's taking off to come up to us." He touched a control on his wrist band and spoke into a tiny microphone. As he spoke, his words boomed from a public address system with speakers apparently throughout the ship: "Shuttle's on its way up. Everyone going down, please get into your suits and have the pressure checked."

The shuttle that came up from the surface of Ceres was quite unlike anything King had seen. Since the planetoid had practically no atmosphere, there was no need for the streamlining, the wings or the controlling surfaces characteristic of shuttles operating from the surface of the Earth or Mars. This was a structure of braced metal girders enclosing spherical tanks and cubic boxes, some of which were fitted with circular windows. Most of the machine's surface was painted a bright, fluorescent yellow, so that it stood out sharply against the star-flecked blackness.

The five passengers were already in their suits, only King and Ferris still without their helmets in place. Ferris looked at the screen showing the approaching shuttle with an expression of horror.

"We travel down in *that*?"

Red Parkes turned to him with a laugh. "That's right. Safer than it looks. Most people from Earth think the equipment looks flimsy when they first come out here, but remember, on the surface of the Earth you have a gravity force equal to an acceleration of 980 centimeters per second squared, right? Here, the surface gravity is only 33 centimeters per second squared—about one-thirtieth as much. You'll be dealing with less violent forces." As if on an afterthought, he added in a lower tone "The physical ones, at any rate."

King wondered what he had meant, but at that moment East's voice over the PA told them to put their helmets in place and check their suit pressure retention, so for the moment further conversation was impossible.

Parkes carefully checked all their suits, switching on their radios. His voice came clearly through a speaker somewhere within King's helmet. "I just want to check your radios. Would each of you answer as your names are called."

There was a chorus of assenting monosyllables, all the radios being linked. Parkes called their names, and each answered. "Busuttil . . . Hannan . . . Ferris, John . . . Ferris, Margaret . . . Ferris, last but not least, Elsa." His attempt at a joke seemed to pass unnoticed.

The yellow shuttle matched spin with the *Karl Friedrich Gauss*, and moved slowly in to the transfer bay where they were waiting. The pilot sat in a transparent glassite globe right forward, wearing a transparent pressure-suit.

"That's a woman flying it!" said Ferris in a note of protest.

"That makes no difference," said Parkes cheerfully. "No time for sex on the way down."

In the burst of laughter that exploded through the radios, Elsa's light soprano seemed to predominate. The shuttle pilot was one of the fattest women King had ever seen. On Earth, she would not have been able to move around. Her body was almost spherical, yet the face that looked out above layered rolls of fat seemed sharply alert.

"Carrying a lot of unnecessary weight, aren't you?" asked King.

"Not in our gravity," said Parkes. "Careful. Your radio's in her range."

"Sorry."

"Their range is just a bit better than a human voice in Earth's atmosphere—remember it that way," advised Parkes.

"Does that apply to all the radios here?"

"Yes. We often want to talk to each other. Without an atmosphere, it's by radio. But we don't want to listen to the combined mumbles of a hundred thousand people. So—limited range."

The passenger compartment of the yellow shuttle was a pressurized cylinder with hemispherical ends, with large windows along the sides. It was built to hold ten people, with five seats on each side of a central aisle. They wore their suits on the way down in spite of the pressurized cabin, apparently as an added precaution.

A screen lit up at the forward end of the cabin, showing the pilot's face. "I'd like you to keep your seat belts fastened," she said, her voice coming through their radios. "The journey down will take only about ten minutes. You'll be landing at Black Plains spaceport. A pressurized vehicle will take you in to Piazzi—a journey of about fifty minutes."

Her image vanished, and was replaced on the screen by a wide-angle view forward from the shuttle, showing the front of the transfer bay. Nitrogen-peroxide jets whistled, and the long, skeletal framework of the shuttle moved slowly back, out into the emptiness of space. They moved astern for a long time, the lighted bay of the *Gauss* growing smaller, until abruptly its main lighting went out.

The positioning jets swung the nose of the shuttle down and to one side. Then a gentle acceleration force pushed them back in their seats as they headed down to the dimly lit countryside below.

Through the window, King was surprised to see a number of extensive green areas, some of them forming broad parallel stripes that seemed to reach over the plains for many kilometers.

"Some of those areas almost look like forest," he

said, forgetting the radio link-up.

It was Gail Busuttil's voice that answered him. "They *are* forests, some of them. Others crops. Grown under plastic domes or half-tubes. The nitrogen comes from Titan."

"From where?" This query came from Ferris.

"Titan. The large moon of Saturn. It has a thicker atmosphere than Earth, nearly all of it nitrogen."

The closer they came to the surface of Ceres, the more alien it looked. In some ways, its scenery was like that of the Earth's Moon—the craters, the ring-walls, the maria —but the similarity weakened on closer inspection. The gravity here was only one-fifth of that of the Moon, and the effects of vulcanism and meteor impact, operating against lighter gravitational restraint, had produced wilder and more spectacular landforms. Some of the crags snarled like fangs.

As the shuttle swung around in a descending curve, King spotted a double straight line of blue lights, with a powerful green beacon away to one side. The pilot's voice came to them.

"If you look down to the left, you can see the lights of Black Plains spaceport. We'll be touching down in approximately three minutes. Please keep your belts fastened."

True to schedule, the craft settled down on its carefully controlled jets, throwing up a cloud of dust from the dark surface, but landing with a scarcely perceptible jar. The jets fell silent, and the dust at once fell to the ground, leaving the surrounding space startlingly clear, so that they could see the jagged cracks in a line of cliffs many kilometers away.

One more check of their suits, and the door of the cabin opened. There was some hesitation, and then Gail Busuttil, who was nearest the door, stepped out and backed down the three metal steps to the ground. The other women followed, and Ferris made an elaborate gesture to King to precede him.

The ground was hard and dead-level—lava that had evidently been artificially ground to a horizontal surface and then vitrified. The shrunken sun, low to the skyline, hung in the black sky like a distant mercury lamp, much whiter than it appeared through the atmosphere of Earth, and three times as far off. Far away across the dark plain, a squat control-tower threw a long shadow.

"It looks—desolate." The words came from Elsa.

"Never mind. It's only the spaceport. They all look desolate." To King's surprise, it was Gail Busuttil who reassured the girl.

Scattered across the spaceport were a number of strangely assorted craft—some of them cylindrical, with pointed noses, standing erect on three or four landing legs, others with open framework like their shuttle. Among them were handling machines, cranes and fork-lifts of what appeared astonishingly flimsy construction. A few hundred meters away a metal railcar stood on a monorail track, the first streamlined object they had encountered since landing.

"Are you all from Earth?" asked the pilot, moving around in front of them. "Except you, of course," she added, gesturing to Gail Busuttil. When the others assented, she pointed to the railcar.

"We're going over there. Remember, you're in one-thirtieth of your accustomed gravity. Watch the way I move, and follow me."

She turned with outstretched arms and faced the railcar, moved one foot forward, and appeared to let herself fall slowly forward on her face. When her bulky body was quite close to the ground, she made a thrust with her leg, sending herself forward in a long, shallow leap. She swung her arms for balance, thrust with her other leg, and went onward in a series of gigantic strides.

King, who had experienced lunar gravity, had little trouble adapting, but each of the Ferris trio made at least one high leap that took them several meters up, out of control. Elsa, making a sudden step to recover her balance, spun upward in a slow somersault. The pilot, hearing her scream, turned.

"Catch her!" she shouted.

King moved quickly to the spot where the girl was going to reach the surface. As she came down, head first, he caught her shoulder and swung her safely to her feet.

"Good save," said the pilot. "Remember, if you split your helmet, the explosive decompression can kill you!"

King held the girl's arm as they continued on their way, releasing her only when they reached the railcar.

"Thanks," she said in a shaking voice.

"It was nothing," said King.

"Don't believe that," broke in Gail Busuttil's voice. "This place isn't a fun park. You could have been dead by now."

"I know." Through her visor, the girl's face looked white.

"Well, thanks," said Ferris. "All's well that ends well, eh?"

"Or some such cliché," said a faint voice over the radios. King didn't know where it came from, nor did Ferris, who looked irritably around in all directions.

The railcar traveled smoothly on its single broad rail, propelled by linear induction. The line ran perfectly straight across the plain towards a ragged line of cliffs that seemed to surround the plain in a vast circle, represented at the far side only by an irregular line of pinnacles rising from far beyond the asteroid's close horizon.

It was strange to travel at high speed across the ground without the sound of roaring wind produced by the vehicle's movement. Once, they ran between long lines of inflated plastic domes with trees growing inside them, sometimes with water sprinkling down on them from high systems of pipes to create artificial rain.

Abruptly, the line tilted down into a cutting, then plunged into a tunnel, traveling on down until it must have been hundreds of meters below the surface. Leveling off, the car slowed in its headlong rush, came to a brightly lit area, and moved slowly through a massive doorway that looked like the opening to a gargantuan safe. It stopped, and the door closed behind it. The whole area was lit by red light, and looking ahead as far as possible, King could see another door.

Suddenly the red lighting became green. The inner door of the airlock opened, and they went through, past a large board with the block-lettered sign WELCOME TO PIAZZI CITY.

Almost at once, they slowed to a stop. "Now," came the pilot's voice over a public address speaker. "We can all get out of our suits. The air here is Earth-normal, but remember the light gravity!"

They went in to a building where space-suits were evidently stored for their owners. There were other exits to the "outside," as the people here described everything outside the city, but to go into space you would have to go through this lock, which led directly to the spaceport.

It gave King a great sense of freedom to get out of the suit. The air didn't seem exactly Earth-normal to him, but it smelt strongly of lemons. He saw the reason for this when he turned and saw a plantation of lemon trees adjoining the building.

Looking up, he saw that they were in a long, semi-cylindrical cavern, perhaps two hundred meters wide, with its ceiling a hundred meters high. Fluorescent lights patterned the distant ceiling, throwing an even radiance over the entire space below.

"It's enormous," said Elsa, wide eyed. "I can't see the end of it."

"There'd be a lot more of it than you can see from here," said King. "A city of a hundred thousand takes up a lot of living-space."

The shuttle pilot moved across to the newcomers like a figure in a slow-motion film. "I'll leave you now," she said. "The same railcar will take you right in to the terminal at Olbers Square. That's the center of the city. There's a hotel called the Solarwide that's good for strangers, right on the central square. You can phone a booking from here, if you like."

She indicated a row of videophone booths against a wall. They were of a distinctive purple shade and a strange design, so that King had not previously recognized them. He strode quickly towards them, his first step hurling him high into the air as he forgot the gravity. Swinging his arms to retain his balance, he at least landed on his feet, letting his knees bend to enable him to take the next, more carefully planned movement.

Reaching one of the booths, he pressed the button for DIRECTORY and tapped out Slade, Anton on the keys. A number came on the screen, and he tapped it out on the numeral keys. Across the screen shone the words NUMBER DISCONTINUED.

He stared at it for a while in disbelief, then went through the performance again. Still, he got the same result.

He found the number for Astrogold (Ceres) Inc. It was apparently still connected, but no one answered his call although he kept it ringing for a full minute.

Again, that unaccustomed feeling of insecurity came to him. He found an address directory key, and was slightly shocked to find Slade not listed. The Astrogold address at least yielded fruit: 9 Hermes Arcade, Level 2, Olbers Square, E. He put the address onto his pocket note-terminal, then walked carefully back to the railcar.

Already, he had the feeling that his search for Slade was going to be more difficult than he had expected.

SIX

The journey to the center of Piazzi City took longer than King had anticipated. Flimsy, roofless houses and apartments lined the rail and the adjacent roadway on either side, rising slightly as they receded towards the arched walls of the great tunnel. It seemed to run on for kilometers, until they suddenly burst out into a vast open space.

The center of Piazzi—and no doubt the original settlement—had been built in a roughly circular crater which had then been roofed over. More than a kilometer in diameter, it might have been covered originally by the standard inflatable plastic dome, but now it was roofed with spidery girderwork on a geodesic pattern, with translucent foam material between the metal rods. Sunlight fell slantingly on one side of it, and the foam diffused the light evenly across the city's heart.

In the darker places between buildings, the natural light was assisted by fluorescent lamps, but to King the overall illumination seemed dim. It was like being in a city at dusk, when the street lighting was late in being turned on. As he emerged from the railcar on to the terminal platform, however, he noticed that most of the people around him had large, wide-open eyes, as though they had adjusted to the low general level of light.

Olbers Square was a surprise to him. In the center of it were luxuriant gardens of tropical Earth vegetation. Looking upward, he saw a network of rain pipes fifty meters in the air, and in one section of the gardens a fine mist of rain was dropping slowly, very slowly, to the dripping leaves.

There were shops around the square—at least, around the two sides of it he could see when he walked along to one corner. The architecture of some of the central buildings was more substantial than he had expected from the flimsy housing on the outskirts, some of them built of laser-sawn stone. The people were lightly dressed, the men and many of the younger women often merely in shorts or briefs, some of the other women in wrap-arounds or tunics.

Their physique bothered him at first. A few, who probably carried out vigorous exercise programs, looked fit and muscular, some even suntanned, obviously by ultraviolet lamps, as they showed the white or yellowish outline of goggles around their eyes. But most of them seemed to have run to fat. Soft fat. It did not sag, as it would have done under Earth gravity, so that in many of them the trunk appeared almost globular. The woman who had piloted the shuttle down was not exceptional. Here, she was probably the norm. Their legs probably would have folded under them had they suddenly been transferred to Earth, but here, where even a heavy individual would have weighed little more than three kilograms, their wasted muscles were quite adequate.

Somehow, as a group, they were distasteful to him. A few overweight individuals would have meant nothing to him, but he felt vaguely troubled by the thought that this soft, bloated physique was the standard shape in a city of a hundred thousand people, and possibly over most of the Asteroid Belt.

He found a bank at the corner of a street running into the square, and changed some of his Intersolar traveller's cheques into the local money, which was still called dollars and cents, although the Ceres dollar seemed to have little relation to any other dollar he knew.

"Where can I get a map of the city?" he asked the girl who passed over his money.

"There's a directory. You could get it at a bookstore on the end of the South Concourse." Her large eyes rolled sidelong to indicate the direction.

The directory, not having a very large area to cover, was quite thorough. He found Hermes Arcade running off the Eastern Concourse on the second level, after finding out how to read the maps of a three-dimensional city. The first level was two levels above where he was standing—all around the square, he saw now, was a second concourse set five meters higher up and some distance back, and above that was another. At the corner of the square he found escalators running up to the higher levels, and also running down—looking over the edge of one, he found a dizzying drop extending far below, with level after level apparently filling the bottom of the crater and running off into the surrounding rock.

Coming out on to the second level, he looked up at a signpost on the corner. The railcar had brought him in to the mid-point of the South Concourse. So the spaceport was just about due south of Piazzi—the outside landscape had been so alien to him that he had not been able to determine which direction the car had taken him.

He found Hermes Arcade which cut into both the second and third levels, with a line of shops on the lower level and offices above. He saw the Astrogold symbol as soon as he entered the arcade, but the door of the office was closed. Looking through the large windows, he could see no sign of activity within. Then a piece of pale gold paper taped to the inside of the glass door caught his attention.

It was a letterhead. The printed top of it read:
ASTROGOLD (CERES) INC. Anton Slade, Managing
Director. And there followed the address and phone
numbers. Below that, the word CLOSED was printed
with a heavy marker, and in smaller lettering the name
"Silvi" and another number. King tapped this number
onto his note-terminal.

The sunlight on the dome was now striking it almost
horizontally. With a start, he remembered some of the
data he had absorbed before making the trip. Ceres had
a "day" of only 9 hours and 5 minutes. Here, they
rounded it out and called it a nine-hour day, using
watches adjusted to their local time. King saw a
jeweller's and watchmaker's on the opposite side of the
lower level of the arcade, and he rode an escalator
down, went in and bought a local watch. It seemed to be
well made.

"Where was this produced?" he asked.

The woman jeweler, who was adjusting the wristband
for him, said "Hirayama," but as he hadn't the faintest
idea where that was he didn't pursue the matter.

He found a public phone in the arcade. Like the ones
back near the airlock, they were all identifiable by a particular shade of purple. Glancing at the number on his
note-terminal, he punched out the digits.

It was now dark outside the dome, but the interior
lights had stepped up their output to maintain the same
level of illumination as before. Suddenly the screen lit
up—colored, but two-dimensional—and a fat, blonde
woman looked out at him.

"Silvi," she said, tapping a forefinger against her
breast-cleavage.

"My name is Kingston Hannan. I'm trying to locate
Anton Slade."

"You, too?" She gave a tired smile. "I don't think I
know you. What did you wish to see him about?"

"I'm from Astrogold, head office, Earth."

"Oh, that's different." She was obviously one of the
asteroid-born people. Her skin was very white, like the
under skin of a shark, although her large eyes looked

surprisingly dark, an effect augmented by the dark blue makeup surrounding them. Her creamy hair was cut short. Her face was plump, and she looked as if she had just taken a very deep breath and was holding it, her chest raised, her shoulders lifted almost level with the lobes of her ears. "I'm his secretary and assistant, but I haven't seen him for a quarter of a year."

"Quarter of my year, or of your year?"

"Quarter of our year. That's more than a thousand of our days, or about four hundred of yours."

King frowned. "You mean you haven't seen him for more than an Earth year? Where is he?"

The woman didn't reply straight away. Her eyes explored his face. "I think you'd better come along and see me. Do you know your way around Piazzi yet?"

"I have this." He held up his directory so that she could see it.

"Good. From what I can see behind you, it looks as if you're in Hermes Arcade. Right?"

He nodded.

"I'm out east. Go along to the middle of the East Concourse, and you'll notice a line of electric cars running on a linduc out along the East Corridor. They divide further out, so take a green one, and follow it to stop 39. Right?"

"Got it," he said.

"Get off there, and go to your right. There's a restaurant on the corner. Willa's. All red and yellow. I'll meet you there in twenty minutes."

He walked along the concourse towards the corner of the East Corridor, his directory in his hand, moving with carefully rationed muscular effort to avoid hurling himself high into the air. He studied the crouching, slow-motion lope of the other people moving along the sidewalk, and tried to copy it. Many of them wore crash-helmets. He had noticed this before, and assumed, without thinking about it much, that they had been the riders of motor scooters or some such vehicle. Now, he realized that there were few of these about, all of them electric and quite light. Most of the wearers of the helmets were pedestrians, guarding against an accidental leap or inability to stop in an emergency.

He located the East Corridor, with its line of little electric cars, some green, some red, some yellow. There seemed to be about the same number of each color, but they arrived in a random order, moving at a uniform fast walking speed, some bunched in groups of three or four. At the Concourse end of the Corridor, they swung round in a loop and went back the way they had come.

He saw a few people standing on a low platform alongside the track, and joined them. Several stopped cars by holding a hand in front of them, then stepping aboard. The cars held four people, the double seats facing each other, reminding King of vehicles at a fairground.

He waited behind a fat woman in a metallic blue cape. Beneath the cape, her legs had an almost skeletal thinness, but her hands and arms looked thick and strong, as though they belonged to a different person. She thrust her hand out in front of a yellow car, and some sensor on it apparently picked up the obstruction. It stopped for about ten seconds as she stepped aboard and sat down, then it moved on at the uniform speed of eight or ten kilometers per hour.

The next car was green. King held his hand in front of it, stopped it, and climbed aboard. Smoothly, it went on its way. Normally, the slow speed of the thing would have bored him, but here there was plenty to see. He passed a blue and white building with the sign ICE-BORE, and a logo of a thing like an oil drilling rig. Suddenly, he realized where Ceres obtained its water supply. Water was usually short in space, but here they had enough to grow flourishing gardens. He had forgotten that the carbonaceous chondritic asteroids often contained large deposits of water-ice.

There were a few large commercial vehicles, all electric, moving along the road beside the linduc line, and on one of them, a long tanker, he saw the name Nitro Titan. His mind came back to Anton Slade. Nitro Titan had been Slade's project, bringing nitrogen from the atmosphere of the moon of Saturn. He was really an integral part of this place—yet how could he have disappeared?

He looked at the people on the sidewalk. He could see different Earth races represented—American, Japanese, European, Australian, Brazilian, Indian, and all kinds of permutations and combinations—but always the physique seemed to tend towards the same bulky Ceres shape, and the coloring of the skin bleached out to a pale tint of its ancestral shade. Except, of course, for the minority of obvious fitness fanatics in each group.

The numbers of the stops were clearly visible as black figures on yellow discs standing beside the track on thin poles. They were frequent, and his car did not stop at them, although after a time it slowed as it caught up on the car in front, which in turn had been held up as someone got out of the one ahead of it.

After a few kilometers, the corridor divided into three branches like the pattern of a snowflake, the red cars inclining left, the yellow ones going straight on. King's car went in to the right hand branch, where he saw that all the other cars in sight were green like his. The track extended ahead of him into hazy distance, with flimsy-looking buildings and trees along either side of it. Even the trees looked different here. He recognized Australian citriodora eucalypts, and Japanese cryptomerias, but they seemed taller and straighter and thinner than on their home planet—apparently a combination of light gravity and lack of wind.

The 39th stop was coming up, but even before he spotted it he could see the red and yellow restaurant, a landmark he could not possibly have missed. This was probably why Silvi had chosen it.

He pressed the stop button on the car, and it halted for ten seconds as he stepped out. He was in the middle of a regional shopping center, with many small electric runabouts parked in front of a variety of stores.

He began to move towards the red and yellow restaurant, forgetting the gravity on his first stride and soaring several meters in the air again, swinging his arms in a rotary movement to keep himself upright as he drifted slowly forward and down. Cautiously, he glided forward as the other people did, keeping his feet close to the ground and using very little thrust.

Willa's Restaurant had no outside walls, only slim red pillars holding up an unnecessary but ornamental roof of ornate yellow plastic tetrahedral cells with lights buried in them. Underneath this canopy were round red laminate tables, each supported by a central leg and surrounded by one-piece yellow chairs of what appeared to be molded fiberglass. They, too, looked to King too fragile to be functional, but several people were sitting on them in various parts of the large space.

Nearing the entrance, King tried to slow his approach by normal methods, but his feet skidded on the pavement. He saved himself from crashing into the nearest table only by gripping one of the upright columns with a hastily outflung hand, and swinging himself around it until he got rid of the unwanted momentum.

He looked about the restaurant, which had forty or fifty tables, but couldn't see anyone among the seven or eight people present who looked like Silvi. He turned back to look at the street, and as he did so a small electric runabout came down the corridor and pulled over to park in the side street.

A woman climbed out of it. She wore a large, rounded crash helmet of bright yellow, and thick, quilted jacket of some blue plastic material that made her body look the shape of a barrel. Beneath it were slim, almost spidery legs in thigh-high black boots. As she turned, he recognized Silvi.

She saw him at once, waved, and moved quickly towards him, leaning forward as if she were about to fall on her face, thrusting back with her legs to propel herself. She used the upright columns that supported the roof to direct herself, gripping them with her hands as she passed them.

"You got here sooner than I expected," she said, and put out her hand. As he grasped it, he was surprised by the strength of it. Its surface was calloused as if by hard manual work. Then he realized that, in this gravity, she used her hands more than her feet to move herself about.

The restaurant was set up as a cafeteria. Following the woman's example, King took a tray and loaded it with items similar to the ones she chose. The food was surprisingly varied, a mixture of Japanese, Indian, Lebanese dishes and others he could not identify. The bread looked like whole-grain bread anywhere, but that was the only thing familiar to him.

"I'll fix up for this," said Silvi, and she put her hand into a slot where it was apparently scanned and recorded to charge the food to an account.

"Thanks," said King.

"Don't worry. It's booked against Astrogold."

"Do you charge everything against Astrogold?"

She smiled. "One hand registered for Astrogold, the other for me."

After they had eaten some of their food, sitting at a table in a quiet corner, she pointed to her crash helmet, which she had taken off and placed on a chair beside her.

"You'll need one of those if you're stopping here any length of time. Especially with your leg muscles trained for Earth gravity. You could easily forget where you are and ram your head into a ceiling."

He nodded. "Is that what happened to Anton Slade?"

She frowned slightly, almost as if she didn't know who he was talking about for a second, then shook her head. "Oh, no. He'd been here for more than three of our years, when I lost—lost contact with him. He knew his way about."

King looked about him. "How can you lose contact with anyone in a place like this? I mean, it's a fairly closed community, isn't it?"

She shook her head. "Not altogether. People come in and drift away all the time. There are a lot of ways of making money very quickly and easily in the Belt. Prospecting is the obvious one. Exploring all the thousands of small asteroids. All you need is a low-powered space-boat, a halogen searchlight and radar to find your way among the debris, a UV light to make minerals fluoresce, a magnetic detector, and you're in business. They all *think* they're lucky at the start. Some of them are. Some we never hear of again.''

"Did Slade do that?"

"Actually, I don't know." She looked at King searchingly. "He got into trouble with Astrogold for siphoning off some of their money for a project of his own, didn't he?"

"What made you think that?"

"Well, I *was* his secretary. Astrogold sent a fellow called Edgar to check up on him. An accountant, or auditor, or something."

"Lance Edgar?"

"Yes. You know him?"

"I knew him. He's been with Astrogold for years. I didn't know he came out here."

"Funny they didn't tell you."

"Where is he now?"

"He disappeared."

"He *what*?"

She spread her hands. "Just wasn't around after a certain time. Perhaps he and Slade are exploring the universe together." She lifted her glass. "To absent friends and colleagues, eh?"

King joined her in a half-hearted toast, his mind elsewhere.

"Unless—" said Silvi thoughtfully.

"Unless what?"

"Probably nothing. But—Anton had a very violent temper sometimes. He could flare like something exploding. I don't suppose—no, that's ridiculous."

"Are you thinking Edgar might have found out something the corporation wouldn't approve of, and Slade—knocked him off?"

"You couldn't knock anyone off, as you call it, in a closed city like this. How would you get rid of the person's body?"

"You've got freight vehicles going in and out. Nitro Titan trucks, for a start. I don't think that would be a problem."

"Also," she said, "Slade often went outside for different purposes. So did Edgar, I think, to check on things."

For perhaps a minute, neither of them spoke.

"How did you get on with Slade?"

"All right, up to a point. But he was always secretive. Didn't like anyone prying into his affairs."

"I'd like to have a look through the records back at your office."

"I don't know if I still have the key to it."

"No matter. I can get the lock drilled out."

She took a quick gulp of her drink. "Don't do that. I'll have a spare key somewhere." She looked at her wristwatch. "Tomorrow be okay?"

King shook his head. "I'd rather make it now."

SEVEN

Silvi's runabout made the journey back to the center of the city much faster than the outward run in the linduc car. She had stopped only briefly at her apartment, and emerged within less than a minute with the key to the office.

She parked the runabout in a below-ground, multi-level park, and they rode the escalators up to the office in the arcade. When they went inside, there was a faint film of dust on the tables.

"Very dusty here?" asked King.

"Not at all. Our air's very clean."

He finger-marked the top of a desk. "Then this would have taken quite a time?"

"Quarter of a year," she said.

Some of the filing cabinets were almost empty. All the bills and receipts King could find appeared to be of routine, relatively unimportant nature. Electricity bills, freight charges, equipment purchases.

"I think Edgar took away all the important files to examine them," said Silvi.

"Where did he take them?"

"I've no idea."

King took a piece of paper from the bottom of one of the file drawers and looked at it thoughtfully.

"What's Mjollnir?" he asked.

"Me what?"

"Mjollnir." He spelled it out. She shook her head blankly. He walked over to her with the piece of paper.

"It looks like a copy of a consignment note," she said.

"Yes. Lot of stuff taken to something, or some place, called Mjollnir. The biggest item here is *paint*."

She took the paper from him and looked at it with her brow furrowed. "It doesn't seem to make sense," she said. "Black paint, dark brown, and dark blue."

"But look at the quantities of it! Where was it used? What did he do with it? Paint an entire fleet of spaceships?"

"But they always paint them bright colors, don't they? Fluorescent yellows and reds and greens and white. So they're easily seen."

"Did he want to paint some ships so they're *not* easily seen? You know, back on Earth they used to paint battleships gray so they were less visible. In space, it'd be black."

"But why the blue and the brown?"

"Ever done any painting?" When she shook her head, he went on. "You mix dark brown and dark blue —say Van Dyke brown and Prussian blue—and you get a sort of black."

"What else is on that?" she asked. He had taken the paper back from her.

"Rocket fuel. Some rocket parts. Igniters—no, only small quantities, probably replacements." He yawned suddenly. "Well, there's nothing I can do with this stuff. May as well leave the rest till tomorrow."

"You want a lift anywhere?"

"No, thanks. I'm booked in at the Solarwide, just around on the South Concourse. I suppose it's safe to take a short cut through the park?"

"Of course. We never commit our crimes in parks, in

the middle of the city. Only Outside!''

"A thought to keep in mind. I'll see you tomorrow."

The pathway through the park curved in graceful
sweeps among prolific vegetation that looked as if it
belonged on a central Pacific island or the Amazonian
jungle. There were little lakes here and there, crossed by
bridges of obviously Japanese design. In fact, there
were even Japanese stone lanterns, or replicas made
from some stonelike material. The paths themselves
were paved with what looked like white river pebbles,
which must have been an expensive item to import.
Ceres was a long, long way from any rivers.

King emerged on the South Concourse almost opposite the Solarwide, which was a towering structure
that looked as if it had been lifted straight from an
Earth city, rising ten stories towards the dome overhead. Probably it had been designed by an Earth archi-
tect working for a worldwide chain of hotels.

Before going up to his room, King walked in to the
bar, where a few people were sitting at tables watching a
TV newscast on a large set high in the corner of the
room. Casually, he looked at the screen. A moment
later, he was away from the bar and sitting at one of the
small tables, watching the screen, as the news commentator brought him up to date with Ceres politics in one
violent jolt.

"We have with us in the studio today John Barron,
Leader of the Ceres Independence party, who will com-
ment on the riot we have just been watching."

A broad-faced man with steady eyes appeared on the
screen. "What we have seen here today," he said, "is
the culmination of a long history of mismanagement of
the economic system of Ceres—indeed, of the whole
complex of inhabited asteroids."

He paused, his blue eyes scanning an audience in
front of him. Cries of agreement went up from it until
he raised his hand, commanding silence.

"All along," he continued, "an association of Earth
governments has subjected all outlying colonies to rigid
control, without attempting to understand the lifestyles

and problems of the inhabitants. They happily move
whole populations from a less profitable area to a more
profitable one, *always taking the short view*!'' He ham-
mered his fist on the rostrum holding the microphones
in front of him. ''They take no account, no account at
all, of the more complex possibilities viewed by local
people.''

King was suddenly aware of someone beside him. It
was Elsa Ferris. ''I had no idea—'' she began, but King
held his finger to his lips and pointed to the vacant chair
at his table. She slipped down into it, eyes on the screen.

''This winding down of three of our major metal mining projects at the same time is the act that has lit the
final fuse! They don't realize that we of the asteroids,
not decadent Earth, represent the future hope for mankind. *We* are man's first rung on the ladder that leads to
the stars!''

There was a burst of spontaneous cheering from the
unseen audience, and then the picture of John Barron
vanished, replaced by the original commentator.

''And that was the scene at Hirayama at five hours
this afternoon,'' he said. ''It has been confirmed, incidentally, that at the moment Earth is buying no more
gold, vanadium or tungsten from the asteroids. And
now, to sport . . . .''

Someone switched off the set. King turned to Elsa.
''You were saying?''

''I had no idea we were coming to a place where there
was all this strife going on. Dad thought it would be
peaceful out here, like our little Pacific island. That is,
before the hurricane hit us.''

''I think they may have different kinds of hurricanes
out here, Elsa.''

''Yetta never mentioned anything about this in her
letters. By the way, she hasn't shown up, yet. She gave
us a phone number, but we don't get any answer when
we try it. We're beginning to wonder if something's
happened to her.''

''How long has she lived out here?''

''Eight years—*our* years, I mean.''

''Then she'll be all right. Very long chance against

anything happening to her just as you arrive."

"I suppose so." Elsa stood up. "I didn't think of it that way. I'll go and tell Mother."

King nodded, smiling slightly as she left him, sliding her feet in the manner of the Ceres people. He stood up and went in to the bar.

The range of drinks available was wide, but mostly unfamiliar to him. Alcohol on Ceres was strictly illegal. So was tobacco, although marijuana and pan were freely available. The restrictions reminded him of the various states of South India. Sometimes, he wondered if state governments simply put the names of a number of drugs in a hat and drew a few out. He had a blue drink that tasted as if it were strongly laced with caffeine, but he didn't enjoy it much, because it was not what he had expected.

Leaving the bar, he picked up his room key. Number 904. That would be the second top floor of the building, as they numbered here from the main floor. He walked towards the lifts. There was one person waiting—a tall, lean woman in a long black coat, with a high, blond beehive hairstyle. When the lift arrived, she walked through ahead of him. Behind her shoulders, her coat curved over a rounded hump that reminded him of Gail Busuttil. He reached for the lift buttons.

"Which floor?" he asked.

The blonde woman looked at him through large, dark glasses. "Ten, thanks, King," she said.

"Eh? Busuttil! I didn't recognize you." He pressed nine and ten, and the lift moved smoothly upward.

"An improvement?" she asked, pointing to the hair.

He looked at it critically. "I don't think so. You looked more individual without it."

"Good. I hate people handing out machine-made compliments. I don't like it, either, but I was pretty well known around here. For the moment, I wanted to play things quietly."

"Is that enough for a disguise?"

"I think so. Gazelles lengthened my leg bones quite a lot. I'm fifteen centimeters taller than when I was here before. Also—" She lifted her hands and touched her high, salient breasts.

King nodded, keeping his expression non-committal. As the lift slowed to his floor, he said: "By the way, have you ever heard of Mjollnir?"

"Well, yes. But why?"

"What's it mean?"

"It's a word out of the old Norse mythology. It was the mythical Hammer of Thor, their god of thunder. In other words, Mjollnir meant a thunderbolt."

"Thanks," he said, and stepped out as the car stopped. "I'll probably see you down in the restaurant tomorrow."

"No, wait!" she said. She seemed to come to a decision. "Come up to my room for a minute."

He stepped back into the elevator, and it went up to the top floor. She led the way along to room 1003. Like his on the floor below, it faced out over the square.

"Sit down," she said, indicating one of a pair of old-fashioned fiberglass chairs. As he sat, she went across to the dressing table and lifted off the blonde wig, then took off the dark glasses. She unfastened the long coat and turned, standing with her hands in its pockets. Underneath it she wore only a short black skirt slit to the hips up either side. She sat opposite King, her dark eyes looking at him intently.

"I don't like the sound of this Mjollnir thing. Where did you run across it?"

He took the piece of paper from his pocket and handed it to her. "It looks like a consignment note. An enormous quantity of dark paint and some other things delivered to some place called Mjollnir."

"Have you checked the local library yet?"

He shook his head.

Rising, she went across to the phone terminal, leaving the camera inactive. Using the keyboard with practiced skill, she soon had a display of the names of all known asteroids. She rolled them up the screen, then held the ones beginning with M. There was nothing listed of the name Mjollnir.

Next, she tried an index of all the place names on the

surface of Ceres. With a patience that surprised King, she was unperturbed at drawing a blank there, and went on to check the surface names of Pallas, Juno and Vesta. Finally, she switched off.

"Nothing," she said. "I think it's a private name, a kind of code name he must have used with his associates. You know, Anton had a peculiar habit about names. He'd call some new project of his a peculiar name that seemed to have been selected at random. Then, when the thing was an accomplished fact, and everyone could see how the name applied, they realized just how far back Anton had begun his planning."

"Dark paint," said King. "It suggests that he wanted to hide something."

"I know." She looked at him from the corners of her eyes. "Did Max Ashman tell you exactly what triggered the rift between Anton and Astrogold?"

King thought for a while. "Not really. He just said he'd gone incommunicado."

"When it became obvious that the Aura project had flooded Earth's market to the extent that it had wrecked the value of gold from there on out, they gave Anton orders to wind down the project. He had a big stake in it. After all, it was the first time anyone had maneuvered an asteroid from one part of the Solar System to another. Actually, the mathematical and astronomical work was done by other specialists, but Anton was nominally the director of the project, and he had a good flair for publicity.

"He made no attempt to wind down the project, as ordered. The Nelson trick—telescope to the blind eye, and so on. Well, he dispatched three freighters loaded with gold within a space of three months—one of ours, and two he ordered without head office authority. There's still an argument going on about who pays for those voyages."

King felt a surge of anger. "Why the hell didn't Max tell me about this?" he asked.

"I don't know. Perhaps *he* didn't know. He might have been acting under instructions from DiMauro and McLaren. Who knows?"

King went down to his own room. He had a lot of thinking to do. He sprawled out on the bed, staring up at the ceiling, which was patterned in intricate arabesque designs of unlikely-looking blue-leaved vines. Running his gaze along the twining stems, he let fatigue catch up with him. Suddenly, he was asleep. He awoke with the changing light in his room as the sun came in through the eastern side of the great dome. Stiffly, he stood up and stretched. It could hardly be morning already! He looked at his watch, and had a moment of utter disorientation as he looked at the digital figures 2:24. Then he realized that he was in the nine-hour day of Ceres, where the sun rose somewhere about 2:15 and set around 6:45.

He showered—an odd sensation in the low gravity, with the water taking a long time to cascade down his body—and then he put on a pair of shorts, shaved, and went out to the elevator.

On the ground floor, he walked into the restaurant.

"Hi!" called a voice, and he turned to see Elsa sitting at a table with her parents. He stopped and ran through a little mechanical conversation. Ferris didn't ask him to join them, so he sat at a nearby table.

Mjollnir, he thought. The Hammer of Thor! Something that came out of the sky and wrought instant destruction! Could it be a maneuvered asteroid? But surely an asteroid would be discovered long before it was anywhere near Earth's orbit, and some countermeasures could be taken. It couldn't be as simple as that. Suppose the name referred to some weapon—a high-powered laser, for instance, or some really devastating bomb? An Amor-type asteroid might be an excellent way of bringing it undetected within a million or so kilometers of Earth.

He was jerked out of his reverie by a shriek from Elsa Ferris. "Yetta!"

She jumped up and ran towards the door of the restaurant. Waddling into the room was a squat, dwarf blonde less than a meter tall. She wore a loose yellow coat with cape sleeves that made her look as wide as she was high, and her large head seemed to account for nearly half her height. Elsa ran to her and knelt down, putting her arms around her. A pair of stubby arms gripped Elsa's shoulders.

"Pick me up," said the woman. "Like a baby. I'm no weight here."

Elsa lifted her and carried her like an infant towards the table where her parents were sitting. "Put me on the table," said Yetta. Elsa stood her on the end of the table, and she shuffled forward to be embraced by her mother. Elsa turned to King.

"This is my big sister," she said proudly.

At the moment, Yetta was looking at her father. Their faces were on a level. She had heavy, rounded breasts and buttocks, and miniature limbs like those of a very fat baby. Ferris looked slightly embarrassed.

"Welcome to Ceres, Dad," she said. "Now you can relax. Forget about being the boss, and leave it all to Yetta. Right?"

He gave a tremulous smile. "Good to see you again, girl."

"Yetta," said Elsa. "This is King Hannan. He came out on the ship with us."

The dwarf woman turned on inward-pointing feet, and looked up at King with cool gray eyes. "Hi, King. Please excuse our family get-together."

"We were worried," said her mother. "We saw that terrible demonstration on TV, and we thought you might have been caught up in it."

Yetta spun around to face her. "I was there. Des was part of the demonstration. He feels very strongly about self government."

As she spoke, King was watching her father. He turned red, then pale, opening his mouth and then closing it again like a stranded fish.

"Well," said Yetta, turning to King, "I'd better take my team home. May see you again."

"Sure," he said.

He watched them go, Yetta waddling between her mother and sister, her father bringing up the rear with a

stunned expression. He walked across to the bar. The
barman nodded after the family.

"Great little woman, that. She and her man run a
prospecting ship. Go all over the Belt after rare metals. I
think the new shut-down may have hit them hard,
though—it's hitting a lot of people. I think we're in for
a lot of trouble."

"It looks like it," said King. "You know a man called
Anton Slade?"

"Heard of him, of course. Who hasn't? Seen him a
few times. Can't say I know him, though. Come to
think of it, I haven't seen him for a quarter of a year or
more."

EIGHT

After a brief rest—part of the time asleep, part of it lying there thinking—King called up Silvi's number on his note-terminal, got an outside line from his room phone and punched out the digits. Silvi's face appeared, with a surprised expression.

"Silvi," said King, "there are a few other points I'd like to discuss with you about Anton Slade."

"Oh. Listen, I was going swimming today. Why not come along with me. We can talk on the beach."

"The *beach*? Here?"

She laughed. "We have a beach. Specially imported. And a lake with waves. I'll pick you up in half an hour."

The picture went blank. A joke? Brush-off? King shrugged to himself and went down for a coffee. However, within half an hour, Silvi's little blue runabout turned in to the small parking area in front of the hotel.

She drove out along the West Corridor, down a tunnel, through an airlock, along another tunnel and up into what appeared to be an area covered by blue sky. They came out into a long, inflated plastic dome, two kilometers at least in length, its height hard to estimate, because it was not supported by girders but simply by air pressure. She parked on the edge of a beach of fine reddish sand. King found himself looking at a lake in which waves rolled towards the shore, breaking in surf. He stared in disbelief for a while, until he figured out the structure at the far end of the lake. The waves, he saw now, were generated by a pontoon which rose and fell, controlled by a rocking arm linked by a connecting rod to a rotating wheel. It moved in a steady rhythm, sending wave after wave towards the beach.

King picked up a handful of the red sand and let it trickle through his fingers. It was very clean and uniform. Sifted.

"Did they bring this sand all the way from Earth?" he asked.

"Mars. Shorter haul, easier lift-off."

She stripped off her wrap-around and walked down to the water's edge. King dropped his shorts and went into the water in his briefs.

"Not cold at all," he said.

"No," she said, wading out into the deeper water. "They keep it at an even 25 degrees C. That's the ambient temperature right through the city."

"Where's the water come from?"

"Over at the smelting plant—you can just see it through the dome. The lake's actually a by-product of the smelter, its waters spread out to radiate heat away from the cooling water of the plant. It's not the same water that's circulated about the furnaces—they siphon off its heat through a system of heat exchangers."

King waded out until his head and shoulders were just above water, bending his knees and springing up as each slow wave swept past. Silvi swam about him, a white, barrel-shaped figure with thick arms and spidery legs, her hair hidden in a close-fitting cap.

"This is fun," she said. "Anton used to come down here sometimes—he liked to keep fit."

Eventually, they went back to the beach. It seemed strange to King to see a woman with a completely white skin lying on the sand.

"Anton adapted very well to the asteroids, didn't he?"

"He thought there was no place like Ceres. So do I, of course, but I'm biased. Second generation Ceres girl. But Anton thought this was where the future is. He thought someone really bright, like him, had a better chance of growing here than on Earth, where you had so many older people in power, people who'd reached the age where they liked to play it safe. At least, that's what Anton thought."

"Quite a movement here for self-government, isn't there?"

"Oh, the Ceres Independence crowd? I suppose most of us agree with them, basically. We're self sufficient, now."

"Do you know a woman called Yetta Ferris?"

"Yetta? Little dwarf woman? Yes. She goes around with a man called Des Marston. They operate a prospecting boat. She does a lot of the heavy work, I believe —uses an exo-skeleton. You know, an electric-powered frame with arms and legs that makes you ten times as strong as a normal person. Des is very keen on self-government."

"Has he ever worked with Anton?"

"Did once. Hates him, now. Says Anton put something over him. Don't know what it was, but it was something where Des lost a lot of money and Anton made a lot. Course, Anton had the brains and the glands for it."

"Anyone else who might have worked with Anton—or still be working for him?"

"Oh, listen, that could be half the people on Ceres. Where would you start?"

The rapidly sinking sun showed emerald green through the crests of the waves as they curled slowly towards the beach. "I can't get used to this," said King. "The day's no sooner started than it's over."

She dropped him back at his hotel. He went up to the tenth floor and knocked on the door of Gail Busuttil's room, but there was no answer. He went to his own room on the floor below, and phoned the desk to see if they knew when she'd be back.

They told him she had left the hotel earlier in the day.

She had left no forwarding address. He decided to go out, and as he dropped his room key in at the desk the clerk handed him a plain envelope with his name on it. He opened it, and found a handwritten note:

King,
    May be on track of A.S. Have caught freighter to Juno.

                                        Busuttil.

There was nothing else. He phoned the spaceport, and learned that the freighter *Algol* had left orbit for Juno only an hour before. The last shuttle had gone up one and a half hours prior to that, and there had been a woman passenger who had secured a passage at the last possible moment.

Apparently there were no regularly scheduled voyages between Ceres and Juno. The distances between the two planetoids constantly varied, because of their different orbital periods.

He went back to his room with a feeling of intense frustration. The woman must have found out some piece of information that suggested Slade was either on Juno or likely to go there. He had missed a chance of going there. For all he knew, Slade might be launching some bizarre weapon from there.

It was a long time since there had been a major war, but often rumors circulated about fantastic weapons that had been developed, but never used, like the space mirror with a giant coelostat that could focus a searing heat-ray onto places on the Earth's surface. Evolving technology might have made some of these ideas cheaper, more feasible than at the time they had first been planned. Mjollnir, the Hammer of Thor. Hell, he might be still wondering what it was when the damned thing was put into use!

A phone call came through for him. He activated the receiver, and Elsa Ferris appeared on the screen, her eyes wide and appealing.

"King, can I see you for a little while? I want some advice."

"What sort of advice?"

"Can't over the phone."

"Where are you?"

"Near the hotel."

"Can you be in the restaurant in five minutes?"

"Yes."

"See you there."

Now what? Whatever it was, it would be a ridiculous anti-climax after the problems that had been haunting him. He rode the elevator down, and walked through into the almost deserted restaurant. To his surprise, Elsa was already there.

"Care for a coffee?" he asked.

"Yes, please."

When they were seated at a small table in a sheltered corner, she said: "It's terribly good of you to see me like this, King."

He shrugged. "Depends on whether I can be of any use."

"It's about my family, partly."

"Yes?"

"You know about Dad and his island colony, and how Yetta left us eight years ago. Well, she and Des made a lot of money, but now things have gone bad with them. They went out and found big deposits of iridium, or something, and now there's no market for the stuff. They've brought Dad and Mother out here—I hate to think what our fares cost—and now they're almost broke."

"So there's friction?"

"Dad and Des can't stand each other. Yetta sides with Des—I think she really hates Dad and Mother.

Blames them for letting her grow up a dwarf. Out here, it hasn't mattered so much, but she had a very frustrating girlhood, and now that Dad and Mother are here I think it's all re-stimulated.''

"Well, I see the problem, Elsa, but I'm not a psychologist.''

"No, but I thought you were the one person I know here who knows a lot—about different things—"

"Wait a minute." He thought for a while. "You say they have a spaceboat?''

"Yes. But they'd never sell that. That's their living.''

"I wasn't thinking of that. Would they fly me to another asteroid?''

"I don't know. They go prospecting in different directions. If you wanted to go to a particular place, maybe . . .''

"I could pay them very well. Astrogold money, not mine.''

"You'd have to talk to them.''

"Will they all be home tonight?''

"Yes.''

"Give me your address. I'll call in, ostensibly to see how your parents and you are settling in after the voyage. Then—well, from there on I'll play it by ear.''

"Terrific! I *felt* you might be the one who could help.''

After she had gone, King permitted himself a doubtful smile.

That evening, he rented a runabout and drove out to the address Elsa had given him. It was at a place called Lakeview, close to where King had gone swimming with Silvi. In fact, Lakeview was not a suburb, as he had expected, but a blue hexagonal apartment building on a narrow isthmus between two lakes, the one where they had swum, and another, quite close to it, the existence of which he had not suspected. He parked the runabout among a number of others near the base of the tower, and craned his neck to look up at the eighth floor—the top one.

He walked in to the foyer. An airshaft extended the full height of the building. Elsa had said to him "Use the handlines, not the elevator—they're quicker." The foyer was wedge-shaped, cutting in to the center of the building, where a door marked UP indicated the lift, and next to it an emerald green door bore the sign PRESSURE REFUGE in large white letters. Apparently a precaution against puncturing of the outside dome.

Next to the elevator was an open shaft with three ropes of colored nylon running over pulleys near the distant ceiling. Colored red, yellow and white, they ran at different speeds. Gripping the white one—the slowest moving—King was hauled smoothly upward. On each floor, he passed a balcony with a gap in its handrail that would have enabled him to step off. He rode the rope to the eighth floor, and swung easily off on to the uppermost balcony.

The balcony encircled the airshaft, with three doors opening from it. He found one with a nameplate reading DES MARSTON and another, below it, simply YETTA. He pressed the button and waited.

"Yes?" came Yetta's voice, high-pitched and hard.

"It's King Hannan. Just called in to see how the new settlers are fitting in."

"Oh." The door slid open, and Yetta stood in the passage within, grotesquely short and squat in a white, caped dress. "Good of you to come," she snapped. "Come in."

She turned and waddled ahead of him with a quick, exaggerated roll of shoulders and hips. The living room gave a view over the lake, with lights reflected in the water. Ferris stood up.

"Indeed," he said, "as my daughter said, it's nice of you to call." He shook hands with King, who bowed to Mrs. Ferris and Elsa.

"Des will be back soon," said Elsa.

King looked at a picture of a spacecraft on the wall. "That your ship?" he asked.

Yetta moved forward to stand beside him. "That's it. The Argo 4. That's me beside it in my exo-skeleton. I call it Yetta 2. It's two meters high, and enormously strong."

"It looks like a robot," said Elsa.

"It is, in a way. But there's little me inside it. You can see my head."

"Are you lifting off again soon?" asked King.

"Nothing planned," said Yetta. "Hey, little sister, how about some coffee?"

"As you wish, big sister," said Elsa, and went through into the kitchenette.

King looked from one to the other of the parents. "What's your initial impression of Ceres?" he asked.

"Busier than I'd thought," said Mrs. Ferris.

"Confusing, I'd say," said Ferris.

"Excuse me." Yetta bustled out into the kitchen. Mrs. Ferris pointed to a photograph on a table. "That's our—our son-in-law, as it were—Des."

King looked at the photograph in silence. It showed a powerfully built man of about thirty, standing with his hands resting on his hips. His legs had been taken off well above the knees, and he stood upright on a pair of short, padded stumps.

"There's another picture of him in his space-suit," added Mrs. Ferris. "Here." It showed the same man, in a bulky space-suit with a life-support system on his back, and heavily gloved hands. Once again, his heavy body was balanced on short, thickly covered stumps. "He feels being without legs is no disadvantage in his business."

"Claims it's a positive advantage," added Ferris.

"His people came out here with him when he was a small child," his wife went on. "He lost his legs in some accident—a rocket burn, I think—and they decided it would be better to leave him here, as he'd be at less of a disadvantage in low gravity."

"What happened to the parents?" asked King.

"Oh," answered Ferris. "They lost what was left of their money, and went home. Left Des here when he was five years old. Irresponsible, I call it."

There was the sound of the front door of the apartment sliding open. "Here he is now," said Mrs. Ferris.

Marston came along the passage with an apelike movement on gloved hands and the short stubs of legs. Coming into the living room, he saw King and swung himself erect on the two rounded pads, stripping off his heavy gloves and thrusting them into the belt of his tunic. His bare arms rippled with gigantic muscles, and his pale blue eyes glared up aggressively at King.

Ferris made the introduction. Marston padded forward, reached up and gripped King's hand with impressive strength.

"From Earth?" he asked in a deep voice.

"Just arrived a couple of days back," said King.

"Thought so," said Marston.

"Does it show?"

Marston nodded. "The way you're careful not to bash your head into the ceiling."

Yetta emerged from the kitchen and Marston dropped his hands to the floor and spun around to face her. "How did it go?" she asked.

"No damned good—nobody wants platinum. It's as bad as gold." He turned back to King, glaring up at him. "That's Earth for you. Shutting down all the Earth-controlled mining and smelting operations. They're going to kill this whole region of space!" Leaning forward, he lifted his huge hands and slammed them down on the carpeted floor. "They don't seem to realize that this is where the future's beginning!"

"Listen," broke in King. "I'm from Astrogold."

"*What*?" Marston swung forward on his hands, eyes blazing as he looked up at King. "They're the bastards that started the landslide!"

"Now, hold it! I had nothing to do with that. But I think I might be able to help you. With Astrogold money."

"What are you talking about?"

"I want someone to fly me to Juno. You have a ship. You could do some prospecting at the same time."

"Prospecting? Can't sell any of the stuff we've found."

"What's the normal charge for flying someone from here to Juno?"

Marston snorted. "Easy to see you come from Earth. No bloody idea! How far from Ceres to Juno, like how far from New York to Tokyo. It doesn't work like that! Asteroids are all moving bodies, in different orbits, catching up on each other, passing each other. Takes someone who's really experienced in navigating the Belt to work out even an approximation to a thing like that."

"That's why I'm asking *you*."

"Eh?" For the first time, some of Marston's explosive aggressiveness seemed to abate. "Come in here," he said, and swung towards the door, turning to look over his shoulder at the others. "Excuse us a minute." He led the way up the passage to a small room with bookshelves and cassette racks in it. Marston stood in front of a computer with a VDT, placed not on a table but on the floor. He looked sharply up at King.

"Before we start, sit down on the floor," he said. "Getting sick of people towering over me on legs." He waited until King was sitting alongside him on the floor. "Why do you want to go to Juno?" he asked.

"I'm looking for a man called Anton Slade."

"That bastard? Why do you want him?"

King hesitated. "For a start, I think he's dangerous. He made a threat against the corporation."

"What kind of a threat?"

"I think he may be planning shifting an asteroid from its orbit."

"He's already done that—about three times."

"Yes, but he may use this one as a weapon."

Marston whistled. "Against Earth?"

"Possibly. Perhaps Ceres, for all I know."

Marston shook his head. "He wouldn't aim at Ceres. Too many people would get to know about it, and we'd know how to deflect it. But Earth? The velocities would be higher there—around 29 kilometers a second. Hard thing to stop, if you haven't the techniques, the know-how handy." He gave a mirthless laugh. "Not that I'd care much if he fired it at Earth. I was brought here when I was a year old, never went back. Suits me, anyway. I wouldn't be any bloody good in their gravity. But here—"

King nodded. "Give me a cost on a trip from here to Juno."

To his surprise, Marston fished a tiny electronic calculator out of a pocket in his tunic. Leaning his broad back against the wall, he tapped the keys of the instrument for a couple of minutes. Finally, he held it out for King to read the display.

"I'll pay you exactly twice that," King said.

"Are you sure you mean that?"

"Yes. As I said, it's Astrogold's money, and I think it's justified."

"That makes it better." For the first time, Marston grinned.

"It's a deal, then?"

"Right. It's a deal."

NINE

The journey to Juno was long, because the *Argo 4* had no equipment for cryptobiosis. It was one of the most uncomfortable voyages King had experienced, for the ship was not only a prospector's craft, it had been designed by Marston for his own use. He had had it built in Hirayama, the main industrial center adjoining Piazzi. In the control room, the ceiling was less than a meter and a half above the floor, and all the switches and levers were within reach of Marston's arms as he sat with his legless trunk strapped into a kind of padded barrel. Beside it was Yetta's dual control setup, with the controls crowded together in even more compact array, within reach of her stubby arms.

King could not help wondering what would happen if one or both of them were incapacitated. He could not have flown the ship—he simply could not have fitted his two-meter tall body in to the control space.

They learned more about each other on the voyage. He found that each of them had an extremely short fuse. Most of the time they were reasonably poised, but their tempers could explode with practically no warning. He learned that certain memories made them flare.

While Yetta was flying, King and Marston spent hours playing chess. Marston never lost his temper over the game, at any rate. They were fairly evenly matched. King moved faster, and in competition conditions he probably would have been the better player, but Marston was extremely careful, sometimes taking so long to make a move that King's concentration would dissipate. His legs often ached as they played, as they sat in an area too cramped for King to stand erect. Marston sat opposite him with his powerful body sweating in glistening rivulets. He kept a thick towel close at hand, and wiped his arms and trunk frequently. He sat with the two short stumps straight out in front of him. They had been surgically modified to give him round, calloused pads to stand on in low gravity.

They always ate their meals together in the control room, while one or other of them was at the controls, King half lying down with his head and shoulders in the cramped cabin.

Somehow, in this fashion, they reached the dark orb of Juno.

The settlement on Juno was nothing like Piazzi. It was raw and primitive. There was a town, of a sort, under an inflated plastic dome, its largest building a general store. Leaving Yetta in the spacecraft on the plain outside the town, King and Marston went in, wearing their space-suits. As King went along with the slow, Lunar-style leaps, he found that Marston could keep up with him easily, even outpace him, using his hands with heavy external gloves—a scampering, four-footed kind of gallop.

At the store, throwing back the helmet of his suit, King asked if anyone there had seen Anton Slade. There were about eight men in the room, but although some of them exchanged glances no one admitted to seeing Slade.

"One other thing," said King. "Has anyone seen a tall woman with a bald head? Bit of a hump on her back?"

"Ah!" One man held up his hand. "That woman in the black wig. She could have been bald. She definitely had a hump."

"That's the woman the two fellows took away," said his companion.

"*What was that*?" demanded King.

"Outside the airlock. Two fellows grabbed her in her space-suit and took her out to their ship, and away."

"Who were they?"

"Suits on. Nobody knew. Looked like a couple of professional heavies."

"Anybody try to follow?"

"No good. They had a very fast ship. Black job. Not big, but very quick."

"They traced them on the radar," said another man who had not spoken yet. "Reckon they headed out for Hidalgo."

One of the older men looked around. "Hidalgo? That place would have to be the blasted end! Most eccentric roid known, isn't it?"

"No." It was Marston who broke in to the conversation now. "Biggest orbital inclination. Forty-two degrees to the plane of the ecliptic."

"Where is it now?" asked King.

Two or three of the others exchanged glances and muttered calculations. Then one of them pointed to the floor. "Down south," he said. "Away below the Solar System as you see it mapped out."

King and Marston headed out through the airlock. Marston, with his heavy gloves on, moved faster than King with his strange four-footed gallop, and he turned half-way to the *Argo* for King to catch up. At once, he thrust out his arm, pointing with an attitude suggesting great urgency.

King turned. Loping after him were two men, one holding a length of metal bar, another a vibroknife. King dodged the man with the bar, kicking savagely at his leg as he did so. The man stumbled as he went past under his own momentum, and King spread out his arms to ward off the knife.

The man with the bar, apparently no more used to light gravity than King, went staggering on in a wide curve, trying to lose speed. The man with the knife triggered the blade, which blurred in savage movement. He swung it at King, who moved quickly back, circling around his assailant so that he could see both of them at the same time.

Marston came up behind the man with the knife like a springing ape. Reaching up, he caught him by the shoulder and pulled him back and down. He dragged him across to a low wall of piled stones, caught him by the wrist and elbow of his knife-arm, and slammed his forearm down on the wall with an appalling violence. Through the faceplate of the other man's helmet, King saw his face distort in a scream, although he could not hear it. Picking him up as the knife fell to the ground, Marston hurled him away beyond the wall.

The man with the bar was now racing towards Marston from behind, the bar swinging menacingly. Unable to reach them in time, King picked up a stone the size of two bricks from the wall, and hurled it with all his strength so that it passed over Marston's head, striking the other man in the helmet.

The stone rebounded high in the air, and the man's rush slowed. A white snowstorm of escaping air whirled into the vacuum from his helmet, and he rushed away towards the airlock, a vapor trail squirming behind him like a phantom snake. Half way to the lock, he fell.

Marston touched King, pointed to the *Argo 4*, and set off. They continued on without further incident, and within a few minutes were aboard.

"Lift off!" shouted Marston, as soon as he was able to open his helmet. Yetta immediately went to her controls, and when he opened his own helmet a few seconds later King heard fuel pumps already running. They took off their helmets, but did not remove their suits as Yetta lifted off.

"Where to?" she called.

"Orbit, until we do some sums. Then we're going to Hidalgo."

On the external-view screen, the plain dropped away. There were a few other small ships there, and one sinister-looking black one, but there was no sign of any pursuit as they swung away around the ragged spheroid of the planetoid.

"You saved my life back there," said King.

Marston nodded. "And you saved mine, which is more important." He smiled. "More important right now, anyway. I can fly the ship."

King extended his hand, and Marston seized it in his powerful grip.

"Why Hidalgo?" asked King.

"I may be wrong, but I think I've got it," said Marston. "Ever heard of the Dyson Whip?"

"What's that?"

"Technique invented a long time ago by an astronomer called Freeman Dyson. They used it in some of the flypast experiments when they were making umanned explorations of the outer planets, long before anybody came out here. Anyway, the idea is this. Say you want to change the direction of this asteroid." He slid a coffee cup along the floor. "Now, over here is a bigger asteroid, moving this way. Now, you do a part orbit around it, and use the movement of the more massive asteroid to pull the lighter one round like a stone thrown from a sling. See?"

"I see. But why Hidalgo? The thing's away from everything else. You said 42 degrees away from the plane of the ecliptic, didn't you?"

"That's right. You know what I think our boys have done? They've installed rockets in an asteroid—maybe atomic—and whipped it around a more massive roid so it's headed down, away from the ecliptic, to where Hidalgo is at the moment, down near the bottom of its orbit."

"What happens then?"

"They use the Dyson Whip again. Bring it *under* Hidalgo, using under in the sense of south, so that it comes upward again at a steep angle towards the ecliptic. Now, anybody's radar only scans near the plane of the ecliptic. Never forty degrees away. Now, this thing could be coming up on Earth from underneath, as it were, where nobody is ever going to think of looking for it."

"I see." King was silent for a long time. "God! You could be right!"

"It all fits, so far," said Marston. "Now, we'll see what we find when we get closer to Hidalgo. I think we'll find a solid, metallic roid heading almost straight for it."

"What can we do about it?"

"Play it by ear, once we see exactly what's happening."

Hidalgo was a relatively large body, visible a long time before they came to its vicinity. With the unaided eye, they would never have picked it out among the dust-clouds of billions of background stars, but Marston used a flicker comparimeter. He took a picture of the view ahead of them, waited an hour, then took another. He projected the two images on to a single screen, adjusting them to coincide. Then he flickered the images, alternating them. Where the distant stars appeared stable, the nearby object—in this case Hidalgo—seemed to vibrate back and forth.

He repeated the process each hour, day after day, because the voyage was long and monotonous. King felt a vague discomfort about heading downward in this way from the plane of the Solar System. Eventually, they were so far down that the familiar planets became hard to find—instead of seeing them more or less in a line, they were appearing randomly scattered.

They picked up no other ships on their radar—neither ahead of them nor in pursuit. Not even meteoric matter. Down here, space yawned below them as a frighteningly empty gulf.

"I'm starting to realize how people feel when they

have agoraphobia," said Yetta.

"Probably different altogether," said Marston. "Not many people have been down here. Slade and his crew—that's probably the lot."

"And Gail Busuttil, and whoever kidnapped her."

"You know," said Marston. "They might know we're coming."

"How?"

"The two fellows who tried to jump us back on Juno. They could radio."

"Hope you're wrong this time," said King.

Hidalgo was showing an appreciable disc when they found the other asteroid. It reflected very little light. From the sunward side, it looked almost completely black. It had a diameter of at least a kilometer.

Swinging round to slow their forward speed with their rockets, Marston left the *Argo 4* on a course that would bring it round in front of the moving asteroid. As they crossed ahead of it, using no power, there was a single spot of light on its dark surface. Marston switched on the high-powered external telescope and brought the light into focus on the screen.

"Light fanning out from the window of a shack," he said. "Let's move slowly in for a closer look."

Yetta, at the right-hand controls, turned the *Argo* slightly with the positioning jets, then started it moving straight in towards the asteroid, using only the slight thrust of compressed gas so that the change in position was almost imperceptible.

"We'd better do this all very slowly," said Marston. "There's a ship down there. See it?"

"Not yet," said King.

"You can hardly pick it out. It's painted black, the same as their shack. That's what I don't like about it. They don't want to be seen."

"I've got it. Left of the shack. Look, there's a smaller ship near it. And something else there, too—forming an equilateral triangle with the shack and the ships. Girderwork of some sort."

"I see it. Radar scanner. All black. Yetta, drift

around in orbit without using any power until we're below their horizon.''

''Right.''

The jagged, rocky surface of the dark asteroid swung slowly below them, while they watched directly from the ports. There was no sign of any other habitation. As the slow drift of the *Argo* brought the settlement down near the limb of the asteroid, Marston moved to the left-hand controls and suddenly began firing gas jets to deflect the *Argo* from its original path.

For a few seconds, King didn't realize what he was doing. Then he saw that he was moving into such a position that the shack and its associated installations were outlined sharply, as they crossed the horizon, against the million points of light of the star clouds of Sagittarius.

Just briefly, they showed in hard, clear silhouette against the far-off blur of milky light. There was more than one radar dish there—a large parabolic reflector, a rapid-scan unit, and something else they couldn't identify because it was partly behind the big dish. The two black ships showed clearly. The shack was larger than they had thought, as if it had been added to in sections. Then the movement of their ship around the asteroid shut the whole of the settlement from view.

''What's that?'' Yetta's voice was tense.

Ahead, around the curve of the tiny world, a fountain of flame and expanding gases jetted outward. It seemed to come from a point on the irregular, rounded mass of the asteroid just about diametrically opposite the shack.

''Rocket blast,'' said King.

Marston said nothing until their slow movement brought them around within sight of the flame. It speared up for hundreds of meters into the blackness. As they looked at it, it suddenly shut off, leaving rolling masses of dust and gas blurring the sharp pinpoints of light from the far stars.

''I was right,'' said Marston. ''They're moving it for a whip around Hidalgo.''

A thought came to King that brought the chill of

ice to him. "Mjollnir. The Hammer of Thor. Must be nearly a cubic kilometer of rock in the thing."

On this side, away from the sun, details on the surface were harder to pick out, but where the flame had blasted they could make out a dim glow of light. There seemed to be a natural impact crater there, not very large, but quite deep. As they passed over it, they could see, faintly in the starlight, the blast tube of an enormous rocket, pointing straight upward. Four smaller tubes slanted out from the main one, like cannon arranged around an ancient fort.

"See the layout?" said Marston in a hushed voice. "Main propelling tube, and four positioning auxiliaries. The thing is completely self propelling, and navigable—probably controlled by a computer in that shack on the far side."

"Just about opposite, isn't it?" asked King.

Marston, never in a hurry to answer, rubbed his chin. "I'd say exactly opposite. Then the thrust of the rocket wouldn't worry them. Only add a bit of gravity where there's hardly any."

Their movement was carrying them away from the rocket emplacement. "You want to keep this orbit?" asked Yetta.

"No. Better kill it. The less we appear over their radar gear, the less chance of them picking us up. Come around about ninety degrees from the rockets, then match solar orbit with the asteroid. That way, we can get a fix on its exact direction."

When they were stationary in relation to the asteroid, about a thousand meters from its surface, Marston switched the large telescope straight forward in the direction in which they were traveling. He took a picture of the star field ahead, waited twenty minutes, then took another. Then he checked the apparent movement of Hidalgo in his comparimeter.

"Doesn't seem to move much," said King.

"That's because we're moving almost directly towards it. See the change of light? That's because it's revolving."

"Could they really aim this thing at Earth—and hit it?" asked Yetta.

"Yes, if their calculations are good. Possibly even hit a specific point on Earth. Like the Astrogold head office or a capital city. They probably want to take out a specific target, but remember the asteroid that wiped out the dinosaurs!"

King's throat felt dry. "You think an impact of a thing like this could practically wipe the slate clean of life all over the Earth?"

"Might, if it went into the sea and punched down into the hot magma."

"Do you think they realize that?"

"I don't know. They might not. Or perhaps they *do* realize it, and they don't damn well care."

"What'll we do about it?"

Marston shook his head. "Don't know. Have to think of something. Fast. There's no time to get help, or to convince anyone else of the danger."

King looked down at the dark landscape below. "Could we land and sabotage their rockets?"

Marston shrugged. "Could, maybe. But we might be too late. They might have already put the thing on a course that needs only minor correction. Remember, it moves slowly down here. As it gets closer to the sun, it accelerates under Solar gravity, and that makes it more tricky to change its direction or velocity."

He switched on the telescope, focusing it on the disc of Hidalgo. For a long time he said nothing. King looked across at Yetta, but she put a finger against her lips, rolling her eyes in the direction of Marston. King nodded slightly and remained silent as Marston did his thinking.

Abruptly, Marston seemed to come to a decision. He punched out an experimental chart of glowing lines on the VDT. He looked at it for a time, then turned to Yetta.

"I'm going down on the surface. I want you to maintain an orbit so that you're always equidistant from the shack and the rocket installation. Get it? In other words, if you regard the shack and the rocket pit as the two poles you'll be traveling round its equator. Right?''

''What are you going to do—wreck their rockets?''

''Better than that. I'm going to take over control of them.''

''But what good will that do?''

''No good to this asteroid, but a lot of good to Earth.''

From the port, King watched the cloud of residual gases blaze in the weak sunshine as Yetta opened the outer door of the airlock. Then Marston's silver-suited figure emerged, looking grotesquely broad, with its powerful arms and stubs of legs. Gases streamed behind him as he jetted slowly down to the dark ground.

There was almost no gravity on the surface of the asteroid. Marston looked at his compass, but there was no magnetic field to give him direction. He looked carefully at the stars to get his orientation, then rested his heavily gloved hands on the rocky ground and hurled himself forward.

He headed towards the ''pole'' where the rockets were located. Turning the power down very low on his suit radio, he called the *Argo 4*. Yetta's voice answered in a monosyllable.

''Got you,'' he said. ''No louder. Can you see me?''

''Lost you. Show your light a second.''

He raised his signalling flashlight. ''Right,'' said Yetta. ''Give me a flash every few seconds.''

The faint spot of reflected light that was the *Argo* swung down towards the snarling peaks of the horizon. Soon Marston would lose sight of it for a while, but the thought didn't bother him. There had been plenty of times when he had been completely alone, often with no other human being within thousands of kilometers.

''More to your left,'' came Yetta's voice as he flashed his light.

He changed his direction and fixed his attention on two sharp, fang-like crags on the near skyline. Passing between them, he could see what looked like the ring-wall of the crater where the rocket installation was located. On the way, his gloved hand encountered a number of insulated wires snaking across the ground, differently colored. Evidently the control wires linking the rockets with the computer control back in the shack. This made it easier. Following the wires, he reached a gap in the ringwall and looked down on the rockets.

The starlit crater was deserted. He could see the end of the blast tube of the central rocket, heat-stained, vertical. Cautiously, he began to scramble down the inner slope. Nearby, a TV camera stood on a roughly welded tripod. He climbed it and bent the flimsy supporting brackets until it was pointed down at the ground in front of it instead of covering the crater floor.

He found a bank of batteries and a generator on level ground, secured by rough welds to spikes driven into the rock. As he was looking at it the ground seemed to drop away beneath him, and a brilliant light from behind him threw his shadow on the ground.

The main rocket was firing. Marston used his nitrogen jets to drive him back to the ground. The firing lasted about ten seconds, and then there was a brief blast from one of the lateral rockets.

Marston didn't hurry. He couldn't afford to make a mistake here. He took out a star chart on which he had marked the point opposite the one where the planetoid was heading. He couldn't see where they were going, from here, but he could infer it by seeing where they came from.

The batteries apparently supplied power for ignition of the rockets, but the switching must be done by a computer in the shack at the opposite "pole."

Taking a pair of strong pliers from a pocket in his suit, Marston cut each of the wires leading away towards the computer. Then he cut the wires leading to the rocket igniters, and bared the ends. He looked at his star chart, then at the sky, then brought the wires against the terminals of one of the batteries. A jet of blue-white flame leaped from one of the directional rockets. Eyes on the zenith, Marston kept the rocket firing until he could see the sky apparently moving across. Then he broke contact and waited patiently, while the movement he had started went inexorably on.

TEN

In the shack, Anton Slade and his team were at a meal when Marston began firing the directional rocket. They were used to these firings, which had their duration precisely controlled by the computer. Normally, they had absolute faith in their computer, but now, after a time, Slade lifted his head.

"Isn't that blast going on a long time?" he asked.

He was a big man, somewhat like King or Max Ashman, but unlike them he had run to fat.

Eldridge, who had programmed and checked the computer, glanced at his watch. "Evidently a course correction," he said easily. "Probably have the main tube blasting in a few minutes."

They went on eating, although Slade looked only partly convinced. Paranoid, thought Eldridge, his thin lips curving slightly. But perhaps it was a touch of paranoia that had got Slade where he was. He looked up to see Slade's prominent, reddish eyes fixed on him, and returned his attention to his food.

A minute later the main rocket began firing. For a

time, Eldridge imagined he could feel perceptibly heavier because of the forward thrust of the asteroid. Hardly likely, of course. When you worked out the figures, the acceleration should be undetectable.

"The main thrust's going on too damn long, isn't it?" demanded Slade.

Eldridge finished his mouthful of food. "We're getting close to the pivot asteroid. It's quite massive, and it may have one or more small satellite bodies we haven't noticed. That would require an evasion blast."

"I didn't notice the blue light," said Agnew.

Eldridge looked up irritably. "What?"

"The blue light that comes on when the radar is scanning. I didn't see it."

"So?"

"So how did the bloody computer know to fire when the radar wasn't operating to pick up this satellite, or whatever."

Eldridge's long, narrow face developed a bright flush across the prominent cheekbones. "We must have missed the light. Hell's hinges, man, we don't have to keep tabs on the computer all the time."

"Listen!" Slade held up his hand. "The main firing's still going on. That's nearly a minute!" He turned to Agnew. "Better check it out. Run a 3D radar scan. And you—" He turned to Eldridge. "Make sure there's no malfunction in the computer."

"Nothing could go wrong there," muttered Eldridge, but at the same time he rose to his feet and glided over to the computer alcove, while Agnew climbed the flimsy rungs leading up to the astrodome.

The firing of the main rocket went on three and a half minutes—Eldridge had glanced at his watch when he felt it start. It was the longest continuous firing it had made since the project began. He wondered if it had kept on firing of its own accord in defiance of the computer—possibly a stuck contact, or something of the kind, although things like that practically never happened with good modern equipment.

He switched on the remote TV camera that gave an

overview of the whole rocket installation, and when the picture filled the screen he gave an involuntary gasp.

"What's the matter?" demanded Slade.

"Maybe nothing. But the camera's shifted its angle."

"How the hell could it do that?" Slade got up and moved into the alcove. "What's wrong with the thing? There's damn-all to see but rock!"

"Maybe a small meteor hit it."

"Meteor? God, do you believe crap like that?"

"Well—what else?"

"Might be a good idea to find out, don't you think?"

"You mean—go outside?"

"Why not? The exercise'll do you good." He lowered his voice. "Better take a gun with you, just in case someone's playing games with our equipment."

Eldridge climbed into his space-suit, carefully reading the instructions on the airlock door. Agnew called down from the astrodome: "Nothing shows on the radar. Only Hidalgo."

Slade stood below the ladder, feet well apart. "I don't know. I've got a feeling. Perhaps you'd better take the shuttle aloft and have a look around. See what your radar picks up from orbit."

One of the directional rockets fired, this time for eight seconds.

"Which one was that?" demanded Slade.

"I don't know," admitted Eldridge.

"Whadya mean, you don't know? Your lights show which tube's firing."

"I know. But none came on. I was watching."

"*What*?" Slade's heavy brows angled into a steep V. He turned to Agnew. "Better get up in that shuttle right now, and have a good look everywhere. Take Carr with you."

Marston, with years of experience in estimating the relative movements of bodies in space—rocks and spacecraft—was relying on his eye to gauge the path taken by Mjollnir in relation to the pivot asteroid. He followed the wires around the surface until he could see

Hidalgo, now showing as a large but irregular disc of almost complete darkness shutting out the stars.

One more positioning blast, he decided. Then five minutes of the main rocket at full power.

He headed back to the installation and again held leads to battery terminals. A slight twist, a straight thrust, then his task was over. The asteroid beneath him would be on a collision course with Hidalgo. The firing over, he would forestall any reversal of his plan by pulling the igniters out of the rockets and throwing them away into space—easy in this gravity. Then he had only to signal Yetta to pick him up.

He made the positional firing, carefully checked the apparent movement of the star fields, then began the firing of the main rocket again. He looked at his watch, holding the wires against the terminals.

The hard, blue-white radiance of the towering flame of the rocket threw black shadows. As he glanced around, it seemed to him that one of the shadows moved.

Without changing positions, he tensed, then casually shifted so that he could look at the rocks where he had seen the moving shadow. A hundred meters away, among broken ridges, he could just see the helmet and shoulders of a space-suited figure. Where most suits were either silver or bright, fluorescent colors for easy visibility, this one was black.

Flexing his arm muscles, Marston got ready for a spring. The man on the ridge brought up something that might have been a gun and Marston took the wires from the battery. As the fuel pump of the rocket cut out, the flame died, and the blackness of a pit abruptly took the place of the patterns of hard light and shadow.

Keeping low to the ground, propelling himself with his arms, Marston moved away from the batteries towards the ridge behind which the man in black was sheltering. Through a break in the ridge, he managed to get the man's figure silhouetted against the stars. He could see a thin-barrelled gun, evidently a magnetic solenoid pistol, held in his right hand.

He began switching channels on his suit radio, running right along the frequency bands until a loud snatch of speech came to him. He turned back to it, and caught the words, clear and loud: ". . . lost the bastard in the dark."

Another voice, not quite so loud, answered: "Careful. He's probably armed, so wait for us to come around there with light."

Marston crouched behind a rock. The only weapon he had was a small screwdriver in a pocket on the outside of his suit. He studied what he could see of the other man's silhouette. He looked as if he was recently from Earth—he could tell by the way he moved.

Groping in the dark, Marston found a loose piece of rock about the size of his fist. He balanced it on his hand, took careful aim, and threw it at a steep surface of rock near the other man, so that it would rebound near him. Since there was no air, there was no sound as the missile struck, but Marston's ruse succeeded better than he had hoped, because the rebounding stone brushed against the black-clad man's leg.

His reflex made him leap around, obviously forgetting the almost total lack of gravity. He gyrated high above the ground, while Marston moved in close below him. Gradually, the spinning figure slowed its upward flight. Relying on the fact that the man's helmet did not give him a view downward, Marston kept directly under him.

The man in black began flailing his arms with fierce energy to slow the spin, the gun still in his hand. Marston, who had played as a boy in near-zero gravity, waited until he could time the revolutions of the other man's body, hands on the ground and elbows bent. When the instant was right, he sprang, coming up behind the man and gripping the air-pipes leading from his oxygen cylinders up to his helmet.

As their helmets made contact, metal to metal, he heard faintly the other man's scream of rage and panic. He tried to bring the gun over his shoulder to shoot at Marston, but Marston's right hand caught the barrel of the gun. Bright electric sparks flickered as two slugs were fired, but both missed. Marston kept his left arm around the other man's body as they both spun in a dizzying whirl, the rocky ground still several meters below them.

"What's happening to you?" An angry voice shouted over the radio. "Eldridge! Come in!"

"The bastard jumped me in the dark." Marston had the effect of listening to two men speaking simultaneously, one voice coming through the radio and the other through helmet contact.

"Don't fool around! Shoot the swine!"

Eldridge, with a sudden, frenzied effort, brought his left arm back, driving his elbow into Marston's side. Gasping, Marston disconnected one of his adversary's oxygen cylinders and flung it away. Air squirted briefly from the connecting pipe before the valve automatically closed. Eldridge, frantic now, fired the gun again, but with no success. Marston took out his second oxy cylinder, then switched his left hand to the gun barrel and brought his right down to feel for his screwdriver. It was still there.

He thrust it into the self-closing valve on the connecting pipe, sending a snowstorm of freezing air whirling about them.

He heard a screech from the other man, muted by their helmets, its pitch rising, unnatural and weird as the air-pressure dropped in his helmet. He heard another voice over the radio: "God, I know that sound! He's losing his air!"

Marston held on to the gun and the screwdriver until the man's legs stopped their wild thrashing. He held him until they landed gently on the surface of the asteroid. He tore the gun from the limp hand, then reached down and gripped a firm edge of rock. He planted his other hand under Eldridge's back, shifting him until he felt his body on balance. Then, with a gigantic thrust of his arm he sent the black-suited body spinning slowly up into the void, the thin, starlit spiral of the last escaping air following it out of sight.

"Eldridge! What's happening there?" The voice on the radio sounded insistent. If Marston said nothing, someone would come investigating. He tried to remember what Eldridge's voice had sounded like.

"It's okay," he said, trying to duplicate the remembered sound of his victim. "I shot the bastard."

There was a silence for a moment, then he heard a voice speaking off-microphone: "Something wrong. That's not Eldridge."

Marston waited, sweat trickling down his body.

"I think you're right," said another off-mike voice. Then, loud and clear: "Eldridge! What happened?" The tone was of a controlled, icy calm that he didn't like the sound of at all.

"Sorry," he said. "I'm a bit shook up. I'll be okay."

Then he switched off. Somehow, he felt he hadn't got away with it. He looked at his watch, then moved quickly down to the batteries and started the main rocket firing again. Another minute, maybe a minute and ten seconds, should be enough to put them straight on a dead-center collision course with the pivot asteroid.

In the cold glare of the rocket flame, he looked around the area for possible cover in an emergency, and decided on an overhanging slab of rock about fifty meters away. He kept scanning the dark, serrated horizon of the miniature world, not knowing from which direction a threat might come. As the base was on the opposite "pole" of the planetoid, there was theoretically no "shortest route" to his position. They might come at him from any direction.

He had been firing the rocket for just on the minute when he saw something rise above the near horizon—a dark shape, with a thin, irregular crescent of reflected sunlight limning one side of it. Instantly, he broke the connection and plunged the whole area into darkness, keeping his eyes on his chosen shelter as he brought on the sudden night.

Using his small flashlight at low power, he removed the ignition unit from the main rocket and hurled it into the airless sky. Then he dived for his rock overhang, waiting only to pull on his heavy outer gloves. Just as he reached his shelter, a cold, green-white light flooded the whole area from above, its angle changing slowly as the craft from which it was directed swung slowly across the sky.

"The rocket's stopped firing," said a voice through the radio.

"I know that, you fool!" thundered the voice Marston had associated with the leader of the operation. "See anything?"

"Nothing suspicious. Not here. No, wait a minute, something on the radar. Not near here. Another ship, I think, in orbit."

"Move up to it. Keep your guns ready. Make contact—try to board it and see what you can find out about it."

"Will do."

Marston switched to the *Argo's* wavelength and pressed the call button. "Yes?" came Yetta's voice.

"You're going to have a visit from one of their ships. Just heard their radio. Don't try to run for it—they'd have a big edge in speed, and they're armed. Play it innocent. You and King came along here prospecting."

"What about you?"

"You don't know about me. We'll have to play it by ear."

He switched back to the other channel.

ELEVEN

Through a porthole, King watched the approach of the black ship. It had the streamlined look of a machine built for atmosphere flight and planetary landings, probably on Mars or Titan. The ebon paintwork was matt, reflecting practically no light, and no radiance showed from its windows or portholes—apparently it used a complementary color barrier such as green interior lighting and red porthole filters.

A voice crackled through their loud speakers. "Calling *Argo 4*." They had read the name on the outside of the hull. "This is an all-wave broadcast. Will you come in on standard channel lambda and reply?"

Yetta pointed to the microphone. "Better if you answered."

King moved over to the radio, adjusting the microphone as Yetta switched to lambda on the dial. "King here, of *Argo 4*. Can you tell me our precise coordinates here? I'm lost."

"Lost?" The voice sounded cynically doubtful.

"My partner did all the navigating, but he's missing. Fellow called Des Marston. Think it might have been a meteor strike."

"Down here?" The voice sounded amused. "Well, plenty of men go missing through meteor strikes in space. Wonder if it ever really happens that way? Anyway—any objection if we come aboard?"

"No objection—but why?"

"Long time since we saw a new face. Like a talk."

King hesitated, looking across at Yetta. "Why not? I'll open the outer door of the airlock for you."

"Right. We'll use magnagraps to lock together."

The black ship maneuvered alongside. It was longer than the *Argo*, and the massive quadruple rockets at its tail suggested a very high speed capability indeed. The magnetic grapnels clanged on the nickel-steel hull of the *Argo*, slipped for a moment, then locked their grip.

"They needn't know about me," said Yetta. "I'll keep out of the way if they come aboard. I'd be more value as a surprise."

King opened the outer door of the airlock, and through the TV screen he saw the door open on the other ship. A figure in a black space-suit emerged and jetted across, closing the door of the *Argo's* lock. King operated the valve to equalize pressure, and when the green light showed he opened the inner door. Glancing around, he saw no sign of Yetta. He decided he'd have less chance of inadvertently giving away her hiding place if he didn't know it.

The man emerged. He lifted back the black metal outer helmet, but left the inner glassite one in place. His voice came through an internal microphone in his helmet and an external speaker on his chest.

"I'm Carr. We wondered what you were doing around here."

"As I said, prospecting. I lost my partner. He's the one who did all the navigating."

"So you're alone?"

King nodded, spreading out his hands. Carr's broad face was strangely expressionless.

"I think you'd better come over to our ship and take a run down to our base. Our boss wants a word with you."

"Who's your boss?"

"Name's Slade. That's all I know about him."

"Why can't we talk over the radio? I don't want to leave this ship empty."

"I'll look after it. You can go down with Agnew. He's in our ship."

"Wait while I put my suit on."

"Plenty of time." Carr took a solenoid pistol out of a holster on the right thigh of his suit, and checked the charge in its battery. King could see the tiny green spark of light glow.

As he put on his space-suit, King wondered again where Yetta had hidden herself. She must be somewhere in the control room, for she would not have had time to move out of it.

"Ready?" asked Carr as King put on his helmet.

King gave a gesture of assent.

"I'll look after your ship. Go across through the airlocks, and Agnew will take you down to the surface. He might even bring you back, if Slade likes your answers."

"Why shouldn't he like them?"

"Never mind. Get moving."

As King emerged from the airlock into the black machine, Agnew was waiting for him with a drawn solenoid gun of the type Carr had carried. With a neutral expression in his pale eyes, he motioned King across to a metal door which stood open.

"What's this?" asked King.

"A little store-room. I'll have to ask you to ride down to the surface in there."

King looked at the gun, then stepped inside the store-room, which was little more than a meter square, and just high enough for him to stand. It would have been a waste of time at this stage to argue. Agnew closed the door, and a bolt grated.

After a minute or two, King heard the sound of pumps, then the roar of rockets. Acceleration pressed

him against the rearward wall of the cubicle. They were
on their way down to the base.

The journey was quite short. He felt the machine
land, and the sound of the rocket engines died, leaving
an immense silence. A few sharp sounds of contracting
metal rang through the ship, and then the door of the
store-room opened. Agnew stood outside in his black
space-suit, the drawn weapon in his gloved hand.

"Out the airlock," he said in an emotionless voice,
"and across to the lock on the shack."

The dark soil of the asteroid was like coal, crunching
under their feet as they moved on it. Over to the right,
the large radar dish swung silently on its girderwork
tower, and to the left stood another black ship, much
larger than the one they had just left.

The far-off sun was directly overhead in the unmov-
ing sky. The shack, as Agnew called it, was a sprawling
black structure that appeared to have been added to in
sections, with two semi-cylindrical wings spreading
across the dark ground at right angles from one another, linked by a round building of welded metal, sur-
mounted by an astrodome. An outer door of an airlock
swung open in the round building, revealing a red-lit
cubicle within.

"Inside," said Agnew over the suit radio. "Stand
against the corner, facing in."

King moved inside the lock, Agnew crowding behind
him. Something he took to be Agnew's solenoid gun
prodded his ribs through the thick fabric of his suit. The
light changed to pure red as the outer door closed, shutting out the weak reflected sunlight. Air whistled somewhere.

The light turned green, and the inner door swung
open. They stepped out into a brightly lit, circular room
with the appearance of an expensive temporary installation, with control panels and terminals near the walls
and multi-colored looms of insulated wire snaking along
the foot of the wall all the way around. King took off
his helmet.

In the center of the room, a large, broad-shouldered
man with gray-streaked, sandy hair gave a booming

laugh. He was standing with his feet apart and his jaw thrust aggressively forward, his reddish eyes summing up King.

"King Hannan! It's been a long time. So it was you they sent looking for me?"

"You took quite a lot of finding, Anton."

"That's why we decided to save you the trouble." He looked around at the others in the room—Agnew, a thin man, and a big, expressionless giant, who took a vibro-knife out of his pocket and tossed it up, catching it with practiced dexterity. He thumbed the switch on the side of it, and King heard the soft, shrill hum of the vibrating blade. He looked back at Slade.

"First of all, what happened to Gail Busuttil?"

"We split," said Slade. "Half a year ago. Ceres year." He smiled. "Both individuals. But you're an Institute man, you know the way it is."

"How about Lance Edgar?"

Slade looked at the man with the knife. "Do we know a Lance Edgar, Joe?"

The big man shrugged, his eyes still on his knife. "Could be. We meet a lot of people."

"Not out here, though," said the thin, jittery man, who had not spoken before.

"No," said Slade. "Not many people come around out here. A man could go missing, here, drift further south of the ecliptic, and no one would know for sure just when and where." He turned to Agnew, who was standing near the radio console. "Get on to Carr. See what he's found."

Agnew snapped a couple of switches, and Slade moved over to a microphone, standing with his feet apart and his hands on his hips.

"Carr," he said. "Have you found anything?"

Carr's voice came from a loud speaker, clear and thin. "Not yet. Fellow seems to be what he said he was."

"He doesn't look like it to us. To you?"

"Nor to me. But he had a partner, and he said he's gone missing."

"You buy that?"

Hesitation. "Think so. Been someone else in the ship. No one here now. I've been right through it."

"Did you check the hold?"

"Not much in there. I thought they might have had a big strike, and he mightn't have wanted to split it two ways. Only food supplies there. I'll check in more detail if you like."

"Do that. And check their computer. Play back their recent course patterns."

"Right. Oh, there's one thing that's odd."

"What's that?"

"Main controls of the ship. All hand controls. No place for the pilot to put his legs."

"Just a moment." Slade looked at King. "Who was your partner?"

"Fellow from Piazzi called Des Marston."

Slade nodded, his expression relaxing a little. "I know. Fellow with no legs." He turned to the microphone. "That's okay. It checks out."

"Good," came Carr's voice. "I'll get back to you." Back on the *Argo 4*, Carr activated the computer and reviewed the past recent movements of the ship on a VDT. Once, he thought he heard a slight sound in the cabin, and he prowled around, looking behind the control consoles. At last, he decided there was nowhere for a person to hide in the equipment-crowded space, and he went back to the screen.

He checked the air in the ship, then took off his glassite inner helmet, placing it on a shelf alongside his outer helmet where elastic straps could keep it from drifting away.

He moved back to the lock opening into the hold of the ship, looking at the instruments that showed him the hold's air pressure and temperature. When he had gone through there before, on his initial quick check, he had worn his suit.

Yetta, edging open the door of the small locker under the control console, heard him go through into the hold. He left the lock doors open as the ambient pressure and temperature were uniform throughout the ship.

Cautiously, Yetta moved out of the locker and across

to the control console, climbing partly onto it.

Carr's first indication that he was not alone in the ship came as he was climbing among plastic bags containing rock samples. Suddenly the fuel-pump motors of the rockets hummed into life, their deep vibration filling the ship.

For a second, Carr froze. Then, muttering, he whipped his gun from its holster and launched himself at the lock leading to the control area.

At the controls, Yetta sat waiting for him to appear, her hands on the familiar controls. She didn't have to look at them to operate them, and she kept her eyes fixed on the lock door.

Carr appeared at the door. At first, he thought the cabin was empty, and his eyes dilated in almost superstitious fear. Then he saw the small, pink-clad figure half-sprawled over the control console. He raised his pistol.

"What—" he began, but at that instant Yetta fired one of the positioning jets. Carr's forward stride took him off the floor with the ship's sudden movement, and his bare head thunked against one of the I-beams reinforcing the ceiling.

Yetta gave the main rockets a short, savage burst, and Carr spun back to crash against the rear wall of the cabin as the ship lurched forward. A second later, the forward thrust of the braking rockets sent his now inert body flying forward again, his solenoid gun whirling out of his limp hand.

Releasing the strap that held her down, Yetta retrieved the gun and thrust it into the elastic belt of her overalls. Cautiously, she approached Carr. He was breathing heavily, his mouth open, a trickle of blood pumping from his forehead—it did not run down, as it would have done under normal gravity.

She dragged him feet-first to the lock opening into the hold, then went back to the controls and skilfully used short bursts of the rockets to maneuver him by inertia through into the hold. Then she closed the lock by remote control.

She was startled by a voice from the radio Carr had

left in the cabin. It had been flung about by the violent movements of the ship, as Carr had been, and it was some time before she found it.

"Carr!" The voice sounded angry. "What the hell are you playing at out there? Carr! Come in!"

Useless to try to mimic his voice. She turned the sound up to maximum.

"Carr!" thundered the voice, and then she heard it less clearly, as if its owner was speaking off-mike: "Better get up there and see what's happened to him."

"Right," came another voice, or possibly two speaking in unison.

Yetta switched the radio off, then opened the channel on her own unit. In answer to her cautious monosyllable came a non-committal grunt from Marston.

"You okay?" she asked.

"Fine."

"They took King down to their base. I hid, and they missed me. Left a fellow on guard. Tough, but an amateur in space. I knocked him out with his own inertia, doing a dance with the jets."

"I saw it."

"So did they. Sending someone up to investigate."

For a long time Marston was silent.

"Do you read me?" she asked.

"Yes . . . Listen! Remember what that fellow Yakamura told us he did when the pirates tried to board him?"

"You don't mean—"

"Try it! I won't have time to get up there—I can see them on the way up. I think they're all amateurs in this part of space. Do it! Then come down here and pick me up."

Yetta watched the black ship slowly closing in on the *Argo 4*. It maneuvered slowly, uncertainly, as if the pilot was not used to close-quarters work among the asteroids. A voice thundered over the radio.

"Calling *Argo 4*. Carr, are you there? Come in on channel delta."

Yetta waited a few seconds, then opened the channel.

"*Argo 4* here. Your friend is not available at the moment. He's resting."

"*Resting*? Who the hell are you? And what happened to Carr?"

"He had a fall when the ship moved a little. Knocked his head. I suggested he rest a while."

There was a babble of voices off-mike. Then—
"We're coming aboard. Open your outer lock door."

The clang and slither of magnagraps sounded on the *Argo*'s hull. The black ship moved alongside it, airlock to airlock. Yetta swung open the *Argo*'s outer door.

"Ready?" asked Agnew, looking across the cabin at Big Joe.

"Shouldn't take long." With a wink, Joe patted the solenoid gun at his hip. He put on his helmet, while Agnew, at the control console, opened the inner door of the lock. Looking across at Joe, he pointed to the radio channel selector on his left wrist, and made the symbol epsilon in the air. Joe lifted his wrist and adjusted his dial.

"Got you," his voice came raucously over the speaker.

"Don't take any chances," said Agnew. "No matter what she looks like—shoot first! Carr wasn't a dummy, remember."

Joe drew his gun and checked the charge on it. The inner door closed. He checked the pressure. This would be easy. Like shooting a pigeon. He rested his hand on the control operating the outer door of the lock, waiting for the green light, his other hand holding the drawn gun behind his back. Somewhere, he heard a rasping sound from the cables holding the magnagraps, as if there had been a relative movement between the two ships, but he didn't think it important.

The green light came on above the outer door. Joe operated the control, and the door swung open. Then there was a sharp, metallic impact that shook the whole of the ship, staggering him off-balance. With a snarl of fright, he raised his gun.

Something dark and massive knocked the outer door

wide open, and Joe found himself looking straight up the main blast tube of the *Argo 4*. Fuel pumps were whining, the sound coming through metal-to-metal contact. Joe's moment of truth came at the same time as the moment of ignition.

"Christ!" he shouted. Then his body thundered in the white inferno of the airlock like a pea in a whistle.

At the controls, Agnew seized the edge of the console to avoid being thrown across the room. Before he could reach the keyboard, the edge of the glowing, red inner door of the lock sprang open, and a terrible flame swirled in.

TWELVE

"Agnew!" Slade's voice was a clap of thunder. "Agnew! Come in!"

After the brief burst of sound, almost like an explosion, the radio had fallen silent. Slade sprang across to the panel controlling a number of outside TV cameras. He spun dials until a view of the two spacecraft appeared, dimly lighted by the sun. Vast clouds of expanding gases spread in every direction about them, obscuring their shapes even as they watched.

"Des Marston was an odd type of guy," said King quickly. "He booby-trapped the ship so that only he or I could get into it."

Slade turned to the thin man. "That square up?"

The thin man shook his head. "No, it doesn't. Wait till I play back the broadcast."

He ran a tape back, watching a counter, then pressed a couple of buttons. They heard Agnew's voice: ". . . *Argo 4*. Carr, are you there? Come in on channel delta." There was a long interval. The thin man held up a finger and pointed to the speaker. Yetta's voice came over. "*Argo 4* here. Your friend is not available . . ."

"Why the hell didn't you tell me about that?" shouted Slade. He turned to King. "Who was that—Oh, never mind. Take him down and lock him in the storeroom!"

The thin man produced a pistol and held it pointing at King's chest. He jerked his head in the direction of one of the doors opening into the wings of the building. King walked across to pick up his helmet.

"No," snapped Slade. "Leave that."

"Move," said the thin man, gesturing with his gun. King moved.

The tunnel-like wing of the building extended for about forty meters, with plastic walls on either side of its central passage, marked with numbered doors of differently colored plastic. It was one of those general purpose, prefabricated buildings that were sold in modules that could be bolted together like a child's construction set.

King walked right to the end of the passage, the thin man behind him. He stopped as the thin man took a bunch of keys from his pocket and began unlocking one of the doors.

"Listen," said King, "I—by the way, I don't know your name."

"No names here."

"Well, I suppose it's okay if I call you Freckles? Now listen, Freckles—"

"Inside!"

King walked into the square, bare room, and the door was locked behind him. Surprisingly, there was an outside porthole that gave him a view of the landing place outside and a ridge of jagged, meteor-whittled peaks, bathed in the weak, unchanging sunlight. He could not see upward far enough to see what had happened to the ships.

He might have been able to break out of this room easily enough, but without a space-helmet there was nowhere for him to go. In any case, the only outlet seemed to be back through the round room where Slade and what was left of his team were waiting.

A number of insulated wires ran along the outer wall, passing through rubber or neoprene grommets in the dividing walls. A slight movement drew his attention to the lower left corner of the room, where the wires were moving in a regular oscillation. Suddenly, he realized that someone was forcing the protective grommet out of its hole. He took hold of the loose side of it and pulled it clear, sliding it along the wire.

"Who's that?" came a woman's voice quietly through the hole.

King bent forward. "Busuttil, isn't it?"

"That's right. King Hannan? What are you doing here?"

"Guest of our mutual pal."

"Did he want you to partner him?"

"No. That what happened to you?"

"Strangely enough, yes."

"Listen, we'll have to try to get out of here. I'll explain why later on."

"I haven't got my space-suit," she said. "I wouldn't get far."

After the explosion, Marston moved out from the area of broken ridges around the rocket installation, looking up at the sky in an attempt to see the *Argo 4*. With a mixture of feelings, he heard Yetta's voice over his radio.

"I'll keep this short. Show me your light."

He swept his signalling light in a series of traverses across the sky. Finally, a light showed briefly above, and he directed his beam towards it.

"Right," came her voice. "I'll come down for you."

Marston suddenly felt an onslaught of weariness as he waited for her to come slowly down to his shielded pinpoint of light. Cautiously, he withdrew an arm from one of the sleeves of his suit, found his towel, and wiped the sweat from his heavy body. Something occluded a group of stars low down towards the skyline, and he tensed again, stowing the towel in the lower part of his suit and quickly slipping his arm back into the sleeve, flexing his fingers into the inner glove. Putting on his outer gloves again, he crouched, watching for the thing that had shut out the stars.

His heart pounded as he moved closer to it. Then he realized it was the space-suited body of Eldridge, the man he had fought back near the rocket pit, slowly falling back to the surface.

He was disturbed by the fact that he had shut off a human life forever. Certainly, Eldridge had tried to kill him, and only his superior knowledge of local conditions had saved him. That, and the immense strength of his arms and hands. Strange, he thought. He had survived because he was without legs. What did that add to theories of the survival of the fittest?

He moved forward as he saw the outline of the unlit *Argo* dropping slowly down a hundred meters away. He reached the ladder on one of the landing legs, grasped a rung and hurled himself straight up into the lower airlock, closing the outer door manually and pressing the button to bring in the air. As soon as the green light came on and the inner door opened, he took off his helmet and scrambled across to Yetta, flinging his arms around her. They stayed like that for nearly a minute, a violent trembling shaking them in a series of waves until it gradually subsided.

"I wasn't sure we'd get together again," she said.

"Neither was I," he added. Then "I had to kill a man."

She squirmed back so that she could look at his face, and her expression was suddenly hard and triumphant. "So had I. It was them or us. I'm glad!"

He gave her a final hug, then moved across to the controls, still in his suit, and waiting only to shed the bulky life-support unit on his back. He swung the ship up and around in a wide curve, finishing almost between the buildings of the base and the Sun. Then he moved slowly down. Above, the disc of Hidalgo was subtending a frightening angle.

"One thing to do," he said.

"Rescue King?"

"They've probably killed him. No, this thing's going to hit. I'm going to wreck their ship. Then there's no chance of them doing it again."

"But I liked King. Remember, he saved your life."

"He did. Yes. Hell!" Suddenly he picked up the radio. "I'm going to chance it."

He looked up at the ominous globe of the asteroid above, very close to the sun, now, with the sunlight forming a thin, interrupted crescent along one edge of it. Then he opened the channel.

"King! Are you there?"

A voice answered him. "I'm locked in a storeroom here."

"I'll try to get you out. Are you near one of those windows?"

"Yes. Here, watch this."

Something light in color waved in the second porthole from one end of the wing to the left.

"I see it. I'll try to get you out. Wait there."

From the window, King could see the *Argo 4* on its way down. Suddenly, he remembered that his space helmet was up in the round room with Slade. Slade! He always was one jump ahead. He might get out of this yet—unless—

Desperately, he looked around the bare room. It had not been built as a prison. The door was probably not very strong. Turning face-down, hands on the floor in the low gravity, he suddenly drove both feet at the plastic door. It shivered, but held, and he had to somersault to save himself from striking his head against the opposite wall. He started at the wall, next time, hurling himself at the door and crashing both feet into it.

Suddenly he heard a shout out in the passage. "Watcher playnat?"

He answered with another violent kick at the door, and then he heard a key turn in its lock. Freckles stood outside, a gun in his hand. "Up front. The boss wants to see you."

He marched King up to the control room. Slade, busy at a console, looked round, his head thrown back. "What happened?" he snarled, the whites of his eyes showing above the irises.

"Trying to bust out of his flat. Made a bloody big dent in the door."

"No matter." Slade looked at King with a savage smile. "You and Gail Busuttil can have the whole place to yourselves in a little while. No radio, of course, and no space-suits. But you'll have the best possible grandstand view of the crash of an asteroid on the Earth's surface. A dramatic way to go out."

"Listen," said King. "It doesn't matter about us in the long run. But have you realized a thing this size hitting the Earth could wipe out life on the whole planet?"

Slade shook his head. "Not all of it. But I have others being prepared, and other deflection orbits worked out. This is only the beginning."

"But—this is the sort of thing that wiped out the dinosaurs!"

"Not quite. That was accidental. This one is planned."

"But why?"

"You should be able to figure that. Look back along the track of evolution. Once, the highest forms were fish. Just one group gave rise to the first amphibians, and from these branched out all higher forms of life to come later. Similarly, one amphibian species—the Eryops—was the ancestor of all land reptiles. One group of reptiles differentiated into all mammals. Coming nearer to our time, you have the primates. One—man—went onward and upward, whereas the others, the gorilla, the chimpanzee, the orangutan—were a dead end. Now, hormonal engineering and gene manipulation has given us a chance to make another step. It's reaching fruition out in space—but the dead weight of conservative, relatively primitive brains on Earth is holding us back in our reach for the stars."

Slade was sweating as he spoke.

"But it's our background. Our history." King gestured wildly. "You can't wipe our entire past out like that."

"The knowledge? All on tape. Microfiche libraries—we have everything you need to know about Earth in libraries in the so-called colonies."

From where he stood, King could see out through the windows at the side of the circular room. Away across the stony little valley, a line of meteor-scarred pinnacles shone in the unchanging sunlight against the black sky.

"But Earth's our origin. We owe it everything."

Slade took a small nail-file from his pocket and began methodically cleaning his nails. "I don't feel I owe the present population anything," he said. "Not after the deal they gave me. Astrogold, the governments, all of them."

"But you can't blame the whole world for what a few individuals did."

"Why not? Political groups never think in terms of individuals. Neither do the big corporations."

Through the windows, King saw the line of pinnacles turn suddenly dark. Slow, inexorable, majestic, the black shadow moved across the stony plain.

"In any case," said Slade, his back to the windows, "All movements begin with a few individuals. They—"

With shocking suddenness came the darkness.

"*What's that*?" shouted Slade.

In the small glow of light from the consoles and dials, King seized a small table—the only moveable thing within his reach—turned it over and swung the edge of it at Slade. Slade, apparently unconscious, spun in a grotesque somersault across to the far wall.

Freckles had rushed to the window nearest him. Launching himself after him, King seized him from behind by the scrawny neck and thumped his temple against the edge of the window, taking the gun from his hand and throwing him aside like a doll.

While at the window he looked out, and the sight

almost paralyzed him. Above, like a monstrous, dark roof, the surface of Hidalgo was coming straight down on them.

"King! King!" The sound came from his suit radio.

He switched on his mike. "Better get out from under it, Des. Goodbye. And good luck. Remember me to Yetta."

"I'm getting you out—you've got one minute."

King looked around. He rolled Freckles over, found his bunch of keys, and raced down the passage. The third key of the bunch of eight opened the door of Gail Busuttil's room. She stood inside, dressed only in a flimsy blue tunic.

"What—" she began, but he seized her wrist.

"No time. Explain later." He dragged her at a frantic, sliding, no-gravity equivalent of a run up the passageway.

"Where did they put your suit?"

"In there, I think." She pointed to an alcove next to the airlock. He helped her into the suit, and retrieved his own helmet from where he had left it on entering. He was just putting it on when Gail Busuttil shouted a warning. Someone grabbed him from behind and hurled him across the room. He struck the wall, rebounding half-stunned.

Slade picked up the gun Freckles had carried, and backed to the airlock. He took his space-suit and helmet from the alcove, and sidled into the lock with the gun still covering them. Before he closed the inner door, King saw him switch the lock to control from within.

"Slade! Wait!" he shouted, but Slade merely shook his head and closed the door.

King turned to the woman. "Where's the main switchboard in this place?"

"I don't know. Yes! Over there!"

At the switchboard, he put his hand on the main fuse. He looked at her. "You know what I'm doing?"

"I know. He doesn't get out, and we don't get out."

"But Earth survives. Am I doing the right thing?"

"Do it!"

He pulled out the fuse. The lights on the dials and gauges vanished, leaving only the faint starlight from the windows.

They drifted towards the window by an unspoken agreement, and he put his arm around her. Above, they could actually see the slow, terrifying downward movement of the other asteroid.

"I didn't think it would all end this way," she said. Her voice was strangely calm.

"I'm sorry, Gail," he said.

They heard a muffled shout, and a frenzied pounding on the door of the jammed and darkened airlock, but they paid no attention to it.

Suddenly, King turned her towards him and kissed her. Her lips were unresponsive at first. Then, suddenly, they were vigorously alive.

THIRTEEN

In the *Argo 4*, Marston was looking alternately at the descending roof of rock above and at the motionless airlock door of the building below.

"Let's get out!" screamed Yetta. "We'll be crushed!"

Marston picked up the microphone. "King! Come out now! Now, or I'll have to leave you."

King's voice came over clearly. "Des, get out! The airlock's jammed, with Slade in it."

Marston didn't answer. He looked at the surface above them, then came to a sudden decision. He started his rockets.

He lifted the *Argo* only a hundred meters above the dark ground, then swung it away from the shack and around behind the tall, projectile shape of the black ship.

"What are you doing?" shrieked Yetta.

"Wait," he said.

He swung the *Argo* back towards the black ship. With

a metallic clang, the landing legs of the *Argo* clawed at
the pointed nose of the other ship. Swinging his ship
almost horizontal, he began increasing the thrust of the
main rocket. Slowly, the black ship began to tilt off vertical, two of its four fins lifting from the ground.

Still embracing, King and Gail became suddenly aware
of a fierce glare of light on the ground outside. King was
not sure, but he thought he could even see reflected
glare on the cratered surface of the other asteroid.

"What's he doing?" he shouted. "He should be out
of here by now."

"Look!"

Then he saw it. The towering shape of the other ship
was leaning further towards them, driven by the
remorseless thrust of the *Argo*'s rocket.

"He's going to crash it on to the other wing of the
building. Quick! Close your helmet!"

With blood-chilling certainty, the ship swung over
and down towards the center.

"King!" came Marston's voice on the radio. "You've
one chance. When the ship hits, get out through the
break in the wall, and rush for the *Argo*. The ladder will
be on the landing leg nearest you. Climb and hang on,
as far up as you can. I won't have time to get you
through the lock until we're clear. Here she comes!"

Things happening outside on the asteroid had been
soundless, but a tremendous crash of sound shook the
building as the forward part of the long hull smashed
down through the prefab wing of the shack. Mixed with
the rending of metal was the hollow boom of the failing
hull, and the swiftly dying shriek of escaping air. Gail
caught King's arm as a hurricane wind hurled them like
blown leaves down the wrecked wing.

For a moment, King thought they were finished.
Then, as they neared the rent in the walls, the fury of the
outrushing air began to abate, as the pressure inside fell.

Throwing an arm around Gail, he lifted both feet and
thrust them against the hull of the fallen ship to stop
their headlong rush. Then, helped by the whistling air,

he threw Gail towards the slash in the wall and crowded through after her into the open.

A white storm of freezing air whirled outside, but he could see the *Argo*. Gripping Gail by the arm, he dragged her towards the nearest landing leg.

"Climb!" he shouted into his suit radio.

Her radio was not switched on. Desperately he half-threw her upward so that she instinctively grabbed the ladder. He climbed behind her, following close to her, forcing her upward until she was against the outer door of the lower airlock. He dragged his way up against her, his arms around her waist and his hands gripping the topmost rung of the ladder.

Either Marston or Yetta must have been watching through the down-looking TV camera, because at that instant the main rocket came to life. Looking down, King saw the flame and dust flying radially out as the ground fell away below them.

Marston climbed only a couple of hundred meters, then tilted the *Argo* over until it was traveling parallel to the ground.

They could not see ahead, because they were in the cavern of the meteor shield. Only a few meters away from them, the main rocket was emitting a frightening blast of white fire that was reflected from the rocky ground over which they sped. The strident scream of the rocket motor was conducted through the metal of the ship, so that they could *feel* the sound through the rungs of the ladder. The radiant heat from the flame began to seep into their suits, especially into King's, as he was slightly lower on the ladder.

The sweat poured down his back, and he found it increasingly difficult to breathe. He felt the flickering of an insane impulse to open his helmet to get air, although his reason told him that would lead only to explosive death.

At last, the rocket shut off. They seemed to be climbing vertically now out of a bottomless chasm, the walls of which were the two colliding asteroids. The gravity of Hidalgo was stronger than that of the asteroid they had left, and rocks and large boulders were now slowly lifting from the ground and moving up towards the larger body.

Far below them, the area of contact lit up with red lightning as the rocky surfaces ground together. Soon the whole bottom of the chasm—the area from which they had leaped to freedom—was lit by a crimson glare of molten rock.

Somewhere down there, in the inferno of unthinkable friction and pressure, was all that remained of Slade, his base, his black ship, and his dream of the next step in evolution.

With the cessation of the blast came the end of the crushing sensation of weight. Above them, at the head of the ladder, the outer door of the airlock swung open. Gail climbed up into the small, red-lit cubicle, squeezed against one side of it, and beckoned to King to follow. He carefully moved up alongside her. He operated the control that closed the outer door, and they stood together, facing each other in the red light as the hiss of incoming oxygen sounded.

At last, the red light in the cramped airlock was replaced by green, and King operated the inner door. The lower lock opened into the hold, and Gail backed into the gloomy space, King following. The lock door closed again under remote control.

King took off his helmet and filled his lungs with the relatively clean air of the ship, watching Gail do the same. They stood looking at each other for a long time in the dim light.

"I didn't expect it," said King. "But we're alive."

She shivered slightly. "On the law of averages, we have absolutely no right to be."

At this moment, the upper lock opened, and Yetta called down to them. "Are you coming up here?"

"Right," said King, and they climbed the ladder to the cabin.

•   •   •

"It's going to be a long, slow trip back," said Marston some hours after their escape. "We used a lot of fuel back there—especially as I hadn't time, in the end, to select a way of escape that pointed towards home. I just had to get *out*."

"You did a very brave thing, waiting to rescue us," said Gail.

"Well, King saved my life a while back," said Marston. He looked at the screen. "Hidalgo's still mostly there, but there's not much left of Slade's roid. They must have had a lot of rocket fuel on the thing. When the tanks blew up, they just about blew it apart." He thought for a while. "Pity about the salvage."

"What salvage?" asked King.

"Their other ship. Lock door blown off, but we could still have got it to Juno. Would have paid for our trip here." He gave a gesture of dismissal. "No good now, though. I wouldn't go in among all that debris."

"You went in among it for us," said King. Suddenly, he extended his hand, and Marston gripped it fiercely.

During the slow voyage back to Ceres—Marston explained several times that he had to reserve fuel for deceleration and landing—the four of them got to know each other as they would never have expected.

Some of the time they played chess, Gail playing the two men simultaneously, and almost always winning both games. Yetta was delighted with this—she would stand with her arm resting on Gail's as she played.

"You're supposed to be on my side," grumbled Marston.

"I like to see a woman winning," retorted Yetta.

"A woman with a built in computer," mused Gail. Her eyes suddenly lifted to meet King's. "Do you mind me having a built-in computer?"

"We're all different, aren't we?" said Yetta thoughtfully. "I wonder if the future's going to be like this? You'd think we didn't belong to the same species."

"Perhaps Slade was right in one thing he said," mused King.

"What was that?" asked Marston.

"He said at each major step in evolution, one most successful life-form went on to differentiate into hundreds of different species as time went on."

"Good. Maybe we're on the way to the future."

FOURTEEN

Max Ashman looked just the same as when King had last seen him, but his first words as King entered were: "You look older."

"I feel older," said King. "People tried to kill me—finally, I had to kill Anton Slade."

"You *what*?" Ashman glared. "That's a stupid sort of a joke."

"Not really. You see—it isn't a joke. It's all there in my report. I don't know whether you'll want to release it as it is, or whether you'd like an edited version. Better read it first."

"I see." Ashman glanced at the report, turning a few pages. He looked up at King. "Anyway, Slade is definitely dead."

King nodded. "Whatever version we release, you can count on that. He's dead. I was there."

"I see. Look, King, we were thinking of resurrecting the Ceres office, running the whole thing differently. It would have worked all right before, had it not been for Anton's megalomania. And I think he may have been influenced by that woman of his—the domehead woman.''

''I think she admits she gave him too much encouragement. She says she learned a lot.''

''Bit late for Slade, eh? Anyway, if you think you could enjoy running the project for a while—or for as long as you like—''

''I'd like to think it over,'' said King.

''Sure. Of course.''

After he had left Ashman, King flew his rented aircar out to Arcturus Lake. He found the tower of jade-green glassite and skimmed in to a landing on the 30th floor.

Before going up to Moya's apartment, he walked down the arcade beside the restaurant to the florist's. They had no green flowers—Moya's favorite color—but he bought some proteas and had them wrapped in a green covering. He rode the escalator up to the 33rd, walked along to 3314, and pressed his hand on the palm plate.

Nothing happened. The bell did not chime within, the door did not slide open. Nothing.

She had taken him off her list of intimates. He thought for a while, and gave the door an old-fashioned knock. Presently he heard her voice.

''Who's there?''

''Hi, Moya. It's King.''

''King who?'' she asked coldly.

He walked back to the escalators and rode them down to the 30th. He walked out to his car, still holding the flowers. Looking up suddenly at her window, he saw her move quickly out of sight around the edge of it.

A man and a woman came to get into the next parked car. He held the flowers out to the woman. ''Would you care for these?''

''But—they're beautiful.''

''Take them, please. I got them by mistake.'' He

drove back to his own apartment, and went in and made a cup of coffee, then sat down to drink it. How long he sat there he had no idea, but when he next picked up his coffee it had cooled to the ambient temperature. He threw it out and was making another when his doorbell chimed.

He opened the door. Gail Busuttil stood there in a long coat and a high, helmet-like hat, all beige.

"How did you find me?" he asked.

"Never underestimate a female domehead." Her dark eyes sparkled. He stood aside and she walked in, pirouetting in the center of the room with her hands in her pockets. "You have good taste, King."

"Good to see you again, Gail."

"And you. What will you be doing?"

He shrugged. "I've been offered the job of running the Ceres operation."

She smiled. "I've had some experience as its midwife. I'd like to try again with a different partner."

Hands still in her pockets, she walked forward until her breasts were almost touching his chest.

"Remember when we were in that room," she said, "with the asteroid coming down on top of us, and we thought it was the finish of us?" He nodded. "Remember the way we kissed?"

"I'll never forget it," he said.

"I'd like you to kiss me like that once more."

Slowly, he put his arms around her, sliding his hands thoughtfully over the smooth computer hump behind her shoulders. Her hat had little dark curls showing under each side, and even the lobes of ears, complete with earrings. Slowly, he lifted her hat off, the synthetic curls and ears going with it.

"I like you as you are," he said. Leaning forward, he pressed his lips against hers. She clung to him, and in his ears was the rhythm of beating wings . . . .

Minutes—or was it hours?—later, they stood at the window looking down over the seething city.

"Will Ashman make your report public?" she asked.

"No. Why upset people by telling them their solid world might have been wiped out?"

"Then most of them will never know what we did for them."

He tightened his arm around her. "The people who matter to us know," he said.

A band of sky above the setting sun was apple green. "By the way, King, there's a special way to make love to a domehead girl."

He gave her a quick hug. "Astrogold's personnel advisers once said I had an exceptional capacity for learning in unfamiliar situations."

She turned around in his arms to face him. It was the first time he had ever heard her break into spontaneous laughter.

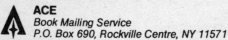